Killer Instinct

Barbara Winkes

ISBN: 978-1-0696671-4-4

For D.

Chapter One

The wind had picked up, making a howling noise as it swirled the snowflakes around. You wouldn't let your dog out in this weather. The ice crystals felt like tiny shards against the unprotected skin of her face, arms and legs. She was almost surprised to see no blood...but wait, there was blood, staining the thin shirt across her side and stomach. Christina gagged at the sight, almost surprised by it at the same time.

What happened?

There were only fractures of images, and sensations. Pain. A soul-eating fear like she had never known before. A warm light. Tender hands. Pain.

Nothing made sense, not her staggering down this ravine during a snowstorm, the way she was dressed, or the blood. Yet, those were the only clues she had, and they amounted to one imperative: *Run!*

No, she wasn't running, but every foot she could put between her and the evil could tip the scale, increase her chances of surviving.

"Come with us, sweetie."

"This will be one night you'll never forget."

"You are special, Christina. That's why we chose you."

The soft, sweet voices in her head didn't leave her alone. Christina shuddered from more than the merciless cold. Somehow, she knew she would never get warm again, not in a million years, even if by some miracle she could manage to find shelter. The cold was deep inside her, and it was here that she might find her grave, in the ice and snow.

She fell, the impact creating an explosion of pain in her side, making her stomach clench. She didn't get sick. There was nothing left to throw up. With impossible effort, Christina pushed herself to her knees, and then to her feet. There was a crimson stain on the pristine white snow. Christina stood and stared, mesmerized by the sight. She felt so weak, exhausted, the last bit of motivation fueled by fear vanishing quickly.

The sound of an engine roused her from her stupor. *Hide!* one of the voices commanded. There was nowhere to hide. Besides, this could be her chance to escape from hell, one way or another.

"We will always be with you."

She stumbled onto the road and in front of the rapidly approaching headlights of the truck, the screeching sound of the brakes hurting her ears.

A merciful blackness enveloped her, drowning out all of the sounds, from outside and within.

❦

Nate Gibson was looking forward to finishing his last shift before his Christmas vacation. He had saved to take his family on the long-desired trip to the Caribbean, worked as many hours as one could justify being behind the wheel of the trailer truck. His boss had still given him the stink eye when he asked for the time off, but now that it was almost here, Nate couldn't care less. He had earned it. Donna had earned it. They would enjoy every second of it. The kids, Aaron and Shelby, six and eight, hadn't been able to sleep for days, too excited for the big trip.

This would be their first real vacation since their honeymoon. They had struggled through recession and job cuts, but now things were finally looking up. It was their dream come true. As soon as he put the truck in the parking lot, a different life could begin, if only for a little while.

In an instant, his life was drastically changed when he saw the shadow on the road, barely visible in the driving snow. Nate hit the brakes, praying he'd be able to keep the huge, heavy vehicle on the road, and away from whatever suicidal creature he had encountered. He assumed it had to be an animal, a deer maybe. No human in their right mind would be out in his weather. As the truck came to a halt, still on the road, Nate took a deep breath and then got out, only to be drawn into a nightmare.

At first, he thought he'd hit the scarcely dressed woman. He felt for a pulse, a drop of cold sweat snaking down his spine. She was still alive. Nate realized that he'd come to a halt a few feet in front of her, and that her injuries stemmed from something else, a...stab wound? Had she been shot?

It was unlikely for a hunter to be out there at the moment.

The woman's skin was cold to the touch. She might be alive right now, but not for much longer. He had to get her to a hospital. Nate envisioned trying to explain to his boss. It didn't matter. He needed to do something, because there was no way he could go on a happy family vacation if this woman died.

Could he move her? What if she had internal injuries, and he'd make things worse—even kill her? He had to get her out of the cold. Nate hurried to put up a reflective triangle and tried a cursory examination. The blood seemed to come from several superficial cuts and one larger, deeper wound. He picked her up and carried her to the trailer. He got a pillow from the sleeping compartment he put under her head, and a blanket to keep her warm. Within moments, there was a dark red stain, though he assumed that the cold would slow down the blood loss. He took off his jacket and laid it on top of the blanket. Less of a blood loss wouldn't save her if the hypothermia got her first.

Nate called 911 and prayed.

⁂

Joanna would never forget the day she shot and killed Norman Decker. The memory still haunted her, every day, because she could have saved many women's lives, had she done it sooner. She hadn't shared this assessment with the lawyer or the court—her sentence might have been more severe than losing her job and spending a few years in prison. With Decker's widow coming to the courthouse every day, talking to the press and showing off her six-months-old baby, Joanna had been lucky, as public opinion shifted and too many people were almost ready to forget what monster the boy's father had been.

Joanna remembered.

In the present, she was hardly a heroine who had slain a monster, and she didn't feel like one. She was out. Her motivation didn't go much further than working a job that paid enough for rent and booze, and keeping appointments with the parole officer.

She had started smoking again as soon as she left the prison gates. On occasion, she hooked up with women who didn't ask too many questions and didn't expect a call the next day.

She didn't have company the previous night when she came home, just collapsed on the sinking sofa bed in the living room and slept until sunlight woke her. It wasn't a pretty picture—the bottle on the table, the ashtray, and the gun she wasn't supposed to have, next to it. There was a time when she'd passionately opposed guns in the home of depressed, potentially volatile individuals. The subject had caused bitter arguments between her and her father before he wrote her out of the will, though that had been because of her "sinful" lifestyle. Joanna hadn't asked what he meant by that—her being a lesbian or sleeping around too much (or going to prison?).

It didn't matter. She accepted her reality for what it was, but that didn't mean she had to like it, or herself.

Joanna sat up, raking a hand through her disheveled hair. She should probably get something resembling breakfast before getting ready for work, though what she really craved was a coffee black as the night, and a cigarette. There wasn't much time for anything else, and her fridge was empty anyway. She wasn't hungry either. She could grab a coffee on the way if she hurried up and talk one of her co-workers into sharing a smoke if she was lucky.

It was getting colder, she realized a few minutes later on the way to her car. Last night's forecast had called for a snowstorm later today. A gust of wind swirled leaves around her feet, making her shiver in her leather jacket. In some places, the Halloween decorations were still up while others were ready for Christmas. This time of year, with its many holidays and cheerfulness, made her even more short-tempered and thus reclusive. Even before the incidents that sent her life on a downward spiral, she hadn't enjoyed them much—now she wished she could just take time off and head south for a couple of weeks, but she needed to pay the bills.

It hadn't been easy to get a job after her prison sentence. Eventually, she'd been lucky: The friend of a friend, who thought people like Decker shouldn't walk the earth, had hired her for his warehouse, where she spent most of her working hours loading and unloading trucks. She didn't hate it—it kept her mind off things.

Joanna liked that it was physical, something that made her feel more at home in her own body, in control. In the past few years, she hadn't been in control of much.

The snow started to fall again on her way to the warehouse. By the time she arrived, traffic had slowed down almost enough for her to be late. She might have been lucky that the owner got her the job, but her immediate supervisor would surely love to shave a few dollars off her paycheck if she didn't show up on time.

Another aspect of her job that Joanna liked was the monotony, the repetitive tasks. Yes, it was demanding, and currently she was freezing her fingers off even with the gloves, but she could escape the hamster wheel in her head for a while. It kept her sane in a way she never imagined. Joanna didn't begrudge the efforts of IAB that had brought her here. She knew that the Internal Affairs inspector hadn't set out to destroy her career—she just was meticulous, believed in obeying the law by the letter, even if said laws protected a serial murderer's life.

Joanna still didn't understand Vanessa Young, or why they had become something akin to friends in the aftermath. Vanessa had come to visit her in prison, which had been a surprise. Joanna had made it clear that she needed no one, but maybe Vanessa needed her.

In the present, they tolerated and gravitated towards each other. Some mysteries didn't need solving.

Work was a bit slower than usual, due to traffic that forced every driver to slow down, and one truck that hadn't come in yet. Joanna overheard co-workers talking, but she wasn't really listening, not interested in the details. Another neat element: She didn't have to watch her back at every turn. This place was a male-dominated area as the police department had been, but there was nothing new. She had already heard every sexist joke, and the ones who tried initially, gave up one by one when they realized they couldn't get a rise out of her. Or maybe they knew that she had once killed a man when she got so sick and tired of his deep and cruel misogyny she couldn't stand it any longer.

Joanna didn't know the true reason, and she didn't care—the only thing important was that they pretty much left her alone. She had the chance to make a living. Norman Decker was still dead and wouldn't cost the taxpayer another cent, a mild sentence considering all the lives he had taken.

Due to the decreased schedule, she had a few minutes to get a hot coffee from the vending machine in the break room. It was bitter and tasted like that machine hardly ever saw a cleaning, but at least it warmed her. A couple of her co-workers stood talking, ignoring her presence. Joanna didn't want to hear about their latest conquests or how they got away with cheating on their girlfriends.

There were a few key words in their conversation that made her halt, producing a familiar, uncomfortable sensation in the pit of her stomach. It might be the lack of food intake. After her shift, she'd find a diner for something greasy and sweet.

Not my circus.

"That's gotta mess with his fancy vacation," one of the men said. "Apparently the police questioned him...She was barely breathing when they found her. He didn't know if she made it."

Joanna picked up her cup from the counter and forced herself to be sociable.

"Hey. What happened?" Her smile would hardly convince anyone. To her surprise, one of them turned to her and said, "A woman almost ran into Nate's truck. No one knows what she ran from, but it had to be nasty. She was bleeding all over the road."

It could have been an accident.

Not my responsibility.

"Did he say anything else?"

"You have to ask him, but he won't come back before the holidays, unless the cops make him stay here."

"Why would they?"

"I don't know. He said someone stabbed her. Maybe they think it was him."

By now, she could barely breathe. Joanna took a sip of her coffee. It wasn't hot anymore, the bitter brew on an empty stomach sickening. It could be the images evoked.

She didn't know Nate very well. She had heard of his plans to take his family on a vacation. Joanna couldn't imagine him hurting anyone, but nice quiet people sometimes turned out to be serial killers. Like Norman Decker.

She tossed the paper cup into the garbage and went back to her shift, but the effect wasn't the usual one. As the hamster wheel started turning full force, her thoughts revolved around a woman, bleeding, running away from her sure death.

Joanna knew she'd forego the diner. When she got out of here, she would need a drink first.

She felt chilled to the bone, which had little to do with the winter outside.

Towards the end of her shift, the workload picked up after all for which she was grateful. Yet, it seemed like the bubble she had lived in for the past years was irreversibly burst. It wasn't like she never paid attention to the news, or the unbelievable cruelties inflicted on women, but for the most part, she managed to keep the disturbing reality at bay. She had paid her dues. She wasn't willing to take part in a losing game any longer.

This was different, a co-worker of hers unwillingly connected to a crime. Too close for comfort. In the car, she heard the news on the radio. There wasn't much information on the woman. She appeared to have been stabbed and left for death. According to the hospital she'd been brought to, she would survive. The doctors hadn't related any further details.

Joanna knew that the police would be combing the area right now for any hint as to who had hurt her. She didn't envy them. There were too many Norman Deckers out there, and they had the power to haunt beyond the grave.

At home, she showered and changed before going back out. She knew from experience that the weather wouldn't keep the patrons from coming to The Copper Door. They were, like her, determined and desperate, and clinging to a past that was only better in their imagination. The door hadn't been copper in years, and while the place used to be a cop hangout, with the owners changing, it had become a place for cheap alcohol, snacks and hook-ups. On occasion, Joanna appreciated all three, and she thought that tonight might be such an occasion.

She wondered if Nate would be able to scrub the image of the woman out of his head and go on his vacation as planned.

A cigarette would be neat, but even The Copper Door had caught up with the times and banned smoking inside. Joanna wasn't willing to give up the warmth for a smoke. She sat down at the bar and ordered vodka, moments later enjoying the burn of the alcohol warming her from the inside. This was better. She didn't need any sleepless nights over someone else's tragedies anymore. She had promised herself. The bartender put a bowl with salted peanuts in front of her, and on cue, her stomach growled.

"I've been longing for some hot wings all day. Would you share?"

Vanessa Young stood out in this place as usual, too dressed up in the woollen coat over the short dress and the leather boots. Joanna made a face.

"You go outside in these clothes? It's a miracle you haven't gotten frostbite yet."

Vanessa shrugged, unfazed by her words. "One of us needs to have a sense of fashion. No, I'm not cold, but I'm hungry. Do I have to eat the whole plate by myself?"

"Don't worry. I'll help you. How was work today?"

It was a small precinct. She must have heard about the woman Nate had found.

"Hectic." Vanessa sighed. "I guess you heard."

"Yeah. Do you know anything about her? More than they said on the radio, that is."

"There are competent people on the case. That's all you need to know."

"Humor me. Unless you pissed off someone else, and it's a cold war up there."

"It's not." Vanessa rolled her eyes. "You know, most people actually appreciate that we at Internal Affairs do our job. No one likes a dirty cop."

"Yeah. I got that concept."

"I wasn't talking about you. God, I need that drink already."

When the bartender had taken her order and refilled Joanna's glass, she continued, "Be glad you don't have to deal with this crap anymore. This woman? Someone drew lines on her body with a marker and started cutting her. She was lucky, they got interrupted and she got out, nearly ran in front of a truck."

"They?"

"Figure of speech. I don't know that much more, and frankly, I don't plan on finding out more if I can avoid it. I don't do the creepy stuff."

"Yeah, I know. Dirty cops are your specialty." Joanna said it without scorn. They were both aware of their past. They still respected each other, and for some reason neither of them could figure out, they couldn't let go of each other.

Something about Vanessa's words struck her as odd, some little detail that bothered her. The marker.

"Oh no, I know that face. I'm not going to look into anything for you. You are not a cop anymore. Let it go."

"I didn't say anything," Joanna said, irritated. "You started talking about the case. I just want to enjoy some junk food and booze in peace."

"All right, let's do that. See anyone interesting around here?" Vanessa asked, her tone softening.

"For you or me?"

"Both."

Even though Vanessa didn't seem to be the type to frequent a place like The Copper Door, she sometimes ended up bringing home some good-looking guy. Joanna preferred women, though the process was the same—neither of them went on second dates much. Maybe that was where they had bonded: They didn't judge each other. They were long past that.

"Not really."

"How about that lady over there?"

Sometimes, they encouraged each other's bad habits, too. The woman Vanessa had pointed out was wearing jeans and a red top, long dark wavy hair. She gave the old-fashioned jukebox a kick when it failed to give her change back.

Joanna winced. "No. Anger issues. I'm just fine."

"Are you?"

"Catch any dirty cops lately?"

Vanessa stirred her Martini with a somber look.

"You know, you were right. No one talks to me that much anymore. I think you're my only friend. That's sad, when you think about it."

Joanna laughed, though she was still uneasy about the revelation, a memory lingering in her mind, struggling to the surface.

No.

"It's not the quantity that counts," she said.

"It counts a little in this case. I wonder if I should change departments. Then again, I believe in the work I do. I'm not a quitter."

"I agree. You don't give up easily—and no, I didn't mean it that way. I was trying to be nice."

"Oh, you are. I'd be eating those wings by myself if it wasn't for you."

"Or maybe you'd be sharing them with this guy," Joanna nodded in the direction of the tall, muscular man who had just walked in, Vanessa's type.

The Internal Affairs inspector signaled the bartender for another drink before she said, "I don't think so. It's not that kind of night."

It was something they both could agree on.

Chapter Two

V anessa wasn't willing to give up her principles under any circumstances. Joanna had to give her that. She had resented her for some time and was sure the feeling had been mutual. In the end, they had realized they weren't each other's enemy, that in fact their enemies were the same.

She couldn't sleep. It wasn't possible, right? That would be too cruel. She had to see Vanessa again, soon, and asked her to look into some details after all, if only for her precarious peace of mind.

Another time, when she'd been much younger and naïve enough to think she could do her part to change the world, Joanna had caught her first serial killer case. She was hit with reality quickly when it also became one of her unsolved cases, the one that battled for center stage with Decker in her nightmares. She had to admit that the memory had become fainter over time, in over a decade, because there was too much evil in the world.

At some point, it all blended together in one ugly picture. She remembered it more clearly now. The women had been tortured with sharp objects, including pencils and ball pens. She recalled being puzzled about the choice of weapons when the individual in question had a range of tools in his arsenal. Maybe the pens hadn't been part of the torture. They had been used to make the cuts more precise...The first murders had looked erratic, then more and more planned out and staged.

Oh God.

No.

It didn't mean he was back. It didn't mean he ever stopped. It wasn't her job.

She called Vanessa on her cell and landline, and as expected, both calls went to voicemail.

"Call me back when you get this. I need to ask you a favor."

In the past, she would have gone back to the station and look up those files herself, but of course she couldn't do that. It was a question whether Vanessa would be willing to go look for answers that would make Joanna sleep better, but she'd take that chance. If anything, Vanessa could pass on the information to the investigating detectives. Someone had to look into that connection.

That someone wouldn't be her, because she had to be at the warehouse early for the double shift she'd signed up for.

At least, one of the other drivers could give her Nate's number, another avenue to pursue.

Joanna didn't have many illusions left, but if she got this wrong, she'd never be able to forgive herself.

❦

Vanessa called her back later. They missed each other once again, but Vanessa's message was clear: *If it's about the case, I can't help you. Take a vacation.*

Joanna shook her head. Nate wanted a vacation, and see how that turned out. Besides, there was a reason why her co-worker had saved for years to go on his. Those long-term plans were always tricky. Life could screw with you at any given moment.

Even so, she had to do something. She left another message for Vanessa to come to The Copper Door tonight, then called the station and asked to speak to the detective on the case.

Less than a minute later, she heard a familiar voice on the other end of the line. Joanna suppressed a sigh.

"This is Detective Randolph speaking. You have information on a case?"

"Theo, this is Joanna. I need to—"

"Okay, listen, because I'm going to say this only once. Whatever you need, I don't care. We're busy here."

The next moment, the line was dead. Joanna stood, telling herself she shouldn't be surprised. Her former co-workers had each dealt with the situation in their own way. They had thought they knew her. Some might have secretly agreed with her, but on the outside, they all had to save face, couldn't condone her actions. That part she understood. The cutting scorn from someone she had once considered a close friend, still stung. What was worse, she didn't have a chance to pass on the information. Were they looking in the right place?

It was back to plan A.

After her shift, Joanna returned to The Copper Door. She had a beer and stuck to the peanuts this time. For this conversation, she needed a clearer head. Because of work, she didn't have much time to follow the media. It didn't matter. If the police had made progress, they weren't likely to share it with the public, not to tip off the perpetrator. If it was the same asshole she had hunted eleven years ago, she wouldn't worry about that. Nothing had worked so far—it might be time for a different approach.

You're in over your head.

It wasn't something she liked to hear, not even from her own voice of reason. Joanna looked around the bar, willing to shut her out. The woman who had kicked the jukebox yesterday was there, sitting by herself at a table. She caught Joanna looking and crossed her legs, giving a smile that was nothing if not inviting.

It didn't look like Vanessa would see her. Joanna's cell phone rang just when she was getting up to join the woman at her table.

"Hey, I can't make it tonight," Vanessa said. "What did you want to talk about?"

"If you could do this for me: There was this case I worked eleven years ago. He stabbed the women with all kinds of tools and knives—"

"Joanna, stop it. I'm not going down that road."

"There were traces of ball pens and pencils. We weren't sure why, but there could be a connection. Theo won't talk to me, so I trust you to pass this on. They have to look into it."

Vanessa sighed. "Okay. I'll tell him if you leave it alone."

"I swear. I just want to make sure this is taken care of."

"Theo's a good detective. He will look at all the possibilities. Wait, when did you talk to him?"

"A few hours ago."

"Don't do that. Don't do it to yourself, or either of them. It's not fair."

"I'll keep that in mind, thanks."

Joanna disconnected the call, feeling sorry for herself all of a sudden. She hated that feeling. She had an idea what would help make it go away.

She slipped the cell phone into her pocket, picked up her beer and walked over to the "anger issues" woman. Contrary to what she'd told Vanessa the day before, she wasn't always so picky.

"Hello there. Would you mind if I sat here?"

"Not at all. My name is Grace."

How appropriate.

Joanna had made bad choices before and dealt with the result-ing, more or less vague, self-loathing. She was a pro when it came to that. As she got up from the king-size bed in Grace's otherwise modest apartment, she felt a tad dizzy even after only two beers. The sex had been...not worth it. For some reason, Grace's reactions seemed exaggerated and fake. She was attrac-tive, but there was no connection, no chemistry. It all seemed mechanical, the memory making her shudder.

"You won't forget to call me back, right?"

"No way," Joanna said.

Right, there was no way she'd see Grace again, and in her mind, she was already moving on. This kind of thing happened. She had other things to deal with, like the question whether Theo would get over himself and hear her out—these days, or at any point in their lives, ever. Once upon a time, they had worked well together.

"Are you sure you don't want to stay a little longer?" She cast a look outside the window, where the snow was still—or again—coming down. "Damn weather. I should have stayed in Cali when I had the chance—but, on the other hand, I wouldn't have met you."

Joanna answered Grace's hopeful smile with a forced one.

"That's true. I better go before it gets worse out there."

When she left Grace's apartment, it was just after midnight. She should have gone home and catch some sleep, but she felt too restless. She didn't want to go back to The Copper Door, so she chose another, quieter bar, where she ordered a Manhattan that she sipped slowly, undisturbed in her corner booth.

Her instincts seldom betrayed her.

She had known that he would kill again. She had an uneasy feeling about Grace, but that might just be that pesky voice of reason talking.

What the hell were you thinking?

I was horny, and I wanted to stop thinking. About the dead women. The slasher's victims. They had called him that for a lack of specifics in his MO. He must have become more sophisticated over the years—after all he had managed to escape arrest for a long time. Norman Decker's victims. She had managed to rescue Mila Folsom from his clutches, but he was long gone. So they had all thought. Then Mila started to reclaim her life, made new friends, went to parties, and invited a quartet of young women over to her home.

Decker broke in and shot all of them, except Mila, because he wanted her to live with the horror, every day, for the rest of her life.

When Joanna got that tip from an anonymous source, all emotions were turned off for those hours it took to formulate a plan and carry it out. She'd get away with it, wouldn't she? After all he was a killer—who would suspect anything? She sought him out. When he opened the door, she pulled the trigger four times, once for each of the young women whose only fault was that they wanted to enjoy dinner with a friend. Decker, as it turned out, had gotten rid of the murder weapon.

She had cried every night after walking out of Mila's apartment, resenting everyone around her, resenting herself because life went on, indifferent to the atrocities that happened all the time. Joanna stopped crying after Decker was dead, though for some reason it didn't make her feel better. Or Mila. All they felt was the grim relief that Decker couldn't hurt anyone else. The monster, however, had multiple heads, growing back ten for each one you cut off.

Even though she felt slightly dizzy—she should have had real food at some point—Joanna ordered another drink. She didn't want to go home. There was no escape.

Vanessa's argument had been that individuals like Decker thrived on chaos and terror, that it was important not to give in to those impulses, even if most people felt he deserved the fate that met him.

Then there were the widow and the baby. Joanna had little understanding for any woman who would tell another woman what she could and couldn't do with her body. Women who sided with killers, in her opinion, were beyond *any* human understanding. No matter what you found in their history—and often it wasn't pretty, but sometimes there wasn't any hint at all—there had to be some sort of responsibility, some accountability. She knew that many of the men she'd put away received letters from women. Marriage proposals had been exchanged in a couple of cases. There was a certain lure in evil.

Not for Joanna. She had tried and failed to do her best to make it all go away, to help create the kind of world she wanted to live in. Her mother had always said she was a dreamer. Days like this, Joanna missed her more than she resented her for putting her own dreams above all else. She had run away in the dead of night, without warning, when Joanna was ten years old.

She had somehow made it home and onto the sagging couch once more. When Joanna woke, it was light outside, and the sounds from down the streets indicated that the day had started without her, some time ago. It seemed like everyone was doing well without her.

The phone rang, and Joanna picked it up immediately, hoping for news from Vanessa.

"Hi, Jo," the cheery voice said.

Joanna barely kept herself from groaning. *Jo?* Usually, it took a long time before she granted the people around her the right to use a nickname. The caller was nowhere near that category.

"Grace. It's so nice to hear from you."

The other woman was completely immune to her sarcasm.

"I was hoping you would say that. Look, I know we didn't part under the best of circumstances. I'm sorry, my mind was on so many things, but I've finally sorted everything out. Would you give me another chance?"

Joanna raked her hand through her hair. She massaged her temple to ward off the headache she felt forming. Those Manhattans had been a bit much on top of the beers. Not to mention expensive. *Voice of reason, it's not your turn. I know damn well this was one bad idea after the next.*

"Grace, I don't think this is going to work out. I am sorry."

"Are you seeing anyone else? Did you cheat on somebody?"

None of your business. Joanna had the impulse to hit end call, but for some inexplicable masochistic reason she hung on.

"No to both. I just think..."

"One more date, please? I promise my entire focus will be on you, as you deserve."

"One more date. All right."

"Thank you so much, Joanna. I swear to you, you won't regret it."

Joanna was regretting it already, but she kept that to herself.

"I have to go, I have another call," she lied.

"Wait, when can I see you? Tonight at The Copper Door?"

"Sure. See you then. Bye."

She called Vanessa, who, to her surprise, picked up right away.

"If you're free, you can meet me at the coffee shop on 37th. I have half an hour."

"I'll be right there." This was clearly a gift horse from Vanessa she didn't want to mess with. Vanessa didn't express it very often, but every once in a while, Joanna got the feeling that her friend did feel guilty. At the moment, Joanna wasn't above exploiting the sentiment for all she could.

Distantly she wondered how Grace had gotten her number. Then again, she had probably left her cell phone out the other night. She had to be more careful with these things, especially when it came to women with anger issues.

Vanessa was already sitting at a table by the window, a specialty coffee and a donut in front of her. Joanna felt a pang of jealousy at the petite woman who seemed to burn calories like crazy. How did she do that? She wasn't out in the field all that much. Joanna knew that if she wasn't working out on a regular basis, her lifestyle would cost her a lot more, and even so, she was often tired of it all.

"Hey. What's up?"

"You promised me to let it go if I could give you something good, right?"

"Right," Joanna said, her heart beating faster. "You guys are any closer to catching him?"

"Baby steps, but they're going into the right direction. The woman who got away, she said she met the guy at a bar downtown, and they went to a motel. One of the slasher victims was found in the same motel."

"That's not a coincidence. Is he getting nostalgic? Trying to send a message? Could he have a partner, or a copycat? She wasn't found in the motel. Do they know where he planned to kill her?"

"Joanna," Vanessa warned. "Theo and Allison have it covered. This is all you get. Now, have a spa day or go away for a weekend. Don't do anything. I don't want to see you in jail again."

"You didn't seem to mind so much the first time."

"Because the first time you did something incredibly stupid that put our whole division under scrutiny," a male voice said behind her. "Now we care."

Turning around, Joanna realized she'd been ambushed.

21

"Oh, hey. That's a surprise. Yesterday you didn't want to talk to me."

Theo didn't pull himself a chair. He probably enjoyed towering over her. It took a whole lot more than that to intimidate Joanna, and besides, she knew him.

"Maybe I'm worried I didn't make myself clear enough. This is my case. You don't have a case. You don't work for this department anymore. Stay away."

"Would you, or anybody, have thought of looking into a case from eleven years ago? A thank you would have sufficed."

"Thank you, Joanna. Now stay away."

"Be nice." Vanessa sighed. "Theo, sit down, okay? This is not what I had in mind. It was supposed to be a peace mission."

To Joanna's surprise, Theo started to laugh. To her even bigger surprise, it was infectious.

"Yeah, sure, make fun of me. I'll get myself another one of those donuts. Don't kill each other."

After Vanessa left the table, there was silence for long moments. They should have felt uncomfortable but didn't. It might be that her encounter with Grace had taken uncomfortable to a new level. This wasn't so bad in comparison.

Theo seemed to be done yelling at her or reacting with scathing disappointment. Passing on the information, she hadn't hoped for any improvement in their relationship, but if that was a side effect, she'd take it.

"How have you been?" he asked.

Joanna shrugged. "I'm doing okay. I heard it's one of our drivers who found the woman, Nate. He's a good guy. I hope you didn't mess with his family vacation."

"He's not a suspect," Theo said, obviously understanding she didn't want to deepen the subject of her life choices and their consequences.

"So, the woman remembered who took her? Was she drugged? The slasher always used GHB. Did you find the kill site yet?"

"I can't tell you anything about this, except we do appreciate your contribution."

"You agree it could be him?"

"I didn't say that. Look, when we're asking you to stay away, it's not punishment, it's a favor. What's done is done. You can't turn back the clock."

It looked like there wasn't much moving forward for her either, like she was trapped in a time warp. Those hours at the warehouse every day were her only escape, how pathetic was that? That, and she had another date with Grace tonight. Talk about pathetic.

"I'm not trying to do that." Theo's look was skeptical, but she went on. "I mean it. It's a bad coincidence that this involved someone I know. I wanted to help, that's all. Now I'm going to be a good girl and do as I've been told. I'd just appreciate it if we could talk once in a while."

"I shouldn't even be seen in public with you, but apparently you're that irresistible."

Theo knew that his charm wouldn't get him anywhere with her. That had never been the plan, it had been a normal part of their interaction, before the yelling and the disappointment.

"Is that so?"

"Hey, I was hoping you two would make up. If you start making out instead, I'm out of here."

Vanessa sat back down with her second donut.

"Don't worry," Joanna told her. "Mission accomplished."

She beamed, and Joanna caught the look Theo was giving her long-time friend. Really? That was potentially bad news, could harm both of their careers. She knew that Vanessa had a knack for living on the edge. She was almost as bad as Joanna that

23

way, though this came unexpected. They'd have to talk about it. After all, they looked out for each other.

Chapter Three

J oanna had planned to lay out all the reasons to Grace why they should part ways after sharing that one last drink. How come she had ended up in her bed instead? At least the sex wasn't so bad this time. As promised, Grace showed more focus, and genuine appreciation for everything Joanna did. That still didn't mean it was a good idea to walk down that path again.

"I can't wait to see you again," Grace whispered.

"I'll be busy for the next few weeks," Joanna lied.

Also, she couldn't go back to The Copper Door for a while if Grace hung out there as well. Contrary to popular belief, Joanna tended to avoid confrontations rather than seek them out.

"That's all right. I can be patient. Can you stay overnight?"

"No, sorry, I have an early start tomorrow." That was a lie, too, but it was better than to be cruel. Eventually, she hoped, Grace would get the hint.

"A few more minutes?"

"Sure."

Grace snuggled up to her, too close for Joanna's comfort. She couldn't even remember when she'd last gone out with a woman who wanted to cuddle and see her again. The thought made her uncomfortable.

"You know, maybe I can give you a little incentive," Grace said. "Something...even spicier."

Alarm bells were starting to ring. Maybe she was beyond paranoid—beyond saving.

"There's a friend of mine...He'd like to meet you. Maybe hang out with us sometime."

No, she wasn't paranoid, not at all. Joanna bolted upright in bed.

"What the hell are you talking about?"

"You know," Grace said innocently. "Some couples do that. I wanted to have you to myself for a bit, but you'd be perfect..."

"Oh, dear God. No. No way. I think it's better if you didn't call me again." Once again, she gathered her clothes and dressed quickly, chiding herself for not seeing the signs. It had been Grace's motivation all along to find a third party. Joanna wasn't interested in being that person, not if someone gave her lots of money for it.

"Why don't you give it a try? I'm sure you'd like it if you gave us a chance."

"No thanks. I don't do couples." More importantly, "I don't do men. Ever. Forget about it."

"Fine, I get it." Grace gave a deep sigh. "What about us? Can't we meet again, just the two of us?"

If forced to, Joanna would have to confess to a brief fling with a married woman, when she'd just gotten out of prison and her life was a constant source of frustration and regret—that occurrence fit right in at the time. She was a little less desperate these days.

"No. This was a bad idea to begin with. I'm sorry, you'll have to find your third party somewhere else. I am not interested."

To her dismay, Grace wrapped herself into the sheet and followed her out in the hallway. "Joanna, please don't leave like this! What if I leave him?"

"I'll be honest. At this point it doesn't make any difference. I'd appreciate it if you deleted my number from your phone. You shouldn't have it in the first place."

"You never once intended to call me?" Grace asked bitterly, as if Joanna was the person at fault.

"I guess now that you figured that out, we can just stop talking to each other. Good night."

"You have no idea what you're missing," Grace yelled after her. Joanna pretended not to hear her. A straight couple on the prowl. Jesus. She needed to re-evaluate her standards *right now*.

This time, Joanna went home right away and powered up her old laptop. It had barely enough memory to allow her high-speed Internet. She searched for any article and social media communication regarding the woman in the hospital and printed out everything she found.

While the printer was working, she poured herself a glass of red wine from the open bottle in the fridge. Her cell phone rang. Grace. Of course, nothing could ever be this easy.

Joanna turned off the phone and went to pick up the pile of sheets the printer had spat out. She scanned the newspaper articles for a name, got lucky on the third one: C. Danvers. Next, she sorted out the social media information. It didn't take her long to find a public Facebook post mentioning Christina Danvers, including tag, expressing the hope she was okay. From the looks of it, the poster was a female friend. Her profile and pictures looked real—which didn't mean there wasn't an imposter hiding behind it, a man, her would-be-murderer stalking her. Or he could be the woman's boyfriend or husband.

Norman Decker had had a wife and a young child.

Christina Danvers' account was better protected than her friend's, but even so, Joanna found a few pictures and her occupation. She was working as a secretary for a big pharmaceutical company. Would she have access to drugs? Would that be of interest to the killer? He probably had stashed up a long time ago. Joanna made a note on a separate sheet.

Christina had a Twitter account in her own name. The last tweet was some cute kitten video, ten days ago. Had she been missing? If she hadn't missed work, the killer had probably taken her on a weekend, aware of her schedule.

The bar. The motel. These places were eerily familiar to Joanna, even if she hadn't been there in years. It was time to revisit, soon. That other time, he had killed the victim in the motel, but in recent years, the area had changed, a lot more traffic. He probably didn't want to take the risk, had brought Christina elsewhere.

She took out a map and spread it on the table, marking the bar and motel, then the place where Nate had almost run over Christina Danvers. How far had she run? What exactly did she remember? There was only one person who could answer those questions, and getting those answers would jeopardize the fragile cease-fire she had with Theo. Vanessa would criticize her but let it go. Theo had no reason to feel guilty toward her, so he wouldn't let her off so easily.

It was best if neither of them knew, at least unless she got some valuable information. In that case, they couldn't be too hard on her.

Joanna had always hated how the lives of crime victims tended to be dissected in the search for a reason, especially when those victims were women. Some tended to leave out information for the fear of judgment. If there was alcohol and flirting involved, it wasn't much of a reach to assume Christina might have done the same.

Joanna didn't plan to be too stealthy—hers was still a familiar name among the cops of her former division, so trying wouldn't serve her. She realized right away that she knew the officer assigned to guard Christina's hospital room. Good or bad, she'd find out soon. She remembered his name, Thomas Hetfield, though they had never talked much.

"Hi there. I haven't seen you in a while," she said, earning a wary look from him.

"Same here. What are you doing here?"

"I'm sure Theo told you already, but this might be related to one of my old cases. I was hoping I could talk to her for a few minutes." No need to tell him that no one had signed off on this.

"Why would you do that? You're not one of us."

So everyone kept reminding her: There was an "us" that she didn't belong to anymore.

"I'm here to help. Sometimes an outsider perspective helps." The term made her cringe, but hey, whatever worked.

"We don't usually let civilians do the work for us, as you know," he said coolly.

Ouch. That said it in even clearer terms than "outsider."

"Then how about letting me talk to her for a moment, tell her that she did great getting away from the bastard? She needs that right now—and I know what I'm talking about. I'll be responsible."

Hetfield looked uncertain. She was going to play his doubts best she could. "I might not be a cop anymore, and I'm certainly not a therapist, but I've dealt with this kind of monster. It's better now than later that somebody tells her she can get through this."

"I don't know."

"Come on."

He looked around, as if someone who'd reprimand him instantly was already close.

"Five minutes, not a second longer."

"Thanks. I'll buy you a drink at The Copper Door."

"Not necessary. Hurry up."

Christina Danvers was awake when Joanna entered the room, staring at her with suspicion.

"You're not a doctor, nurse, or a cop. I don't talk to reporters."

"I'm not a reporter, but I used to be a cop. I'd just like to ask you a few questions, if that's okay with you."

At the first sight of her, Joanna had almost walked out backwards, accepting that what everyone said was right: She had no place anywhere near this investigation.

"No, it's not okay with me. Who are you? What the hell do you want from me?"

In this case, anger was a good thing, Joanna thought. Anger for a reason could potentially keep you alive. It had helped her.

"I know you've been hurt. I worked on cases like this, and one of them was very similar to yours. We never caught the guy."

"Oh, great. I feel so much better now."

Joanna ignored the sarcasm.

"I want to do everything I can to help rectify that, but the police need your help too. Have you told them everything you remember?"

"Of course, I have. Are you—?"

"I killed a man once," Joanna said.

Christina's eyes widened. "How did you get in here?"

"That man was a serial killer, but he also had a perfectly normal life on the side, a wife and a kid. He was preying on college girls. I'll spare you the details, but I want you to know I'm on your side. You got away. You're strong. You can help us finally put him away and stop the nightmares for many others."

"How can you put him away when you're not a cop anymore?"

"I went to prison, and when I got out, I swore to myself, I don't care, it's not my problem. That was wrong. He is still out there, and that *is* my problem. I will pass on everything to the detectives."

"You have no idea." Christina turned away. "All I wanted was some fun. I never thought..." Her words trailed off. "It doesn't matter."

"It does. Whatever it is you did, nothing in the world could justify anyone hurting you."

"No? You didn't see the looks I got from the cops when I told them I went to a motel with a guy I'd met that night. Hey, I was taking my chances, right? You'd think not every man you meet is a sick psychopath. I'll reconsider that."

"I won't give you those looks. I want him to pay."

"Why do you still care? Is this some kind of item you want to check off the list, to redeem yourself?"

Joanna paused, seeing herself with Decker, hearing his laughter, and then, the gunshots. Faith Rickers, Danielle Montgomery, Shellie Gordon, and Emily LeVaughn.

"It's too late for that," she said. "I'm not saying it's not selfish. I'd sleep better if he was locked away for the rest of his miserable life."

She had oftentimes been conflicted about the death penalty which had been abolished in her home state. When she had walked onto the crime scene that Mila's apartment had become, Joanna hadn't been conflicted at all.

Christina looked frightened, but she nodded.

"Okay. There is something I haven't told the police. I'm really sorry."

"That's okay. You tell me now. I'll take the heat," Joanna promised.

When her call went to voicemail for the fifth time in a row, Grace threw her phone against the wall. Edward's laughter made her even more furious.

"Stop it!"

"Why do you care?" he asked, perfectly relaxed as he smoked his cigarette. "We'll find someone new. It's not that hard."

Grace pouted. "She didn't even want to see me again. I should have never brought the subject up."

"Well, it's too late now," he pointed out. "Have you packed? We're leaving early tomorrow."

"I'm not leaving. There's something she didn't tell me, and I have to find out what it is. She was into it, the second time, I could tell."

Edward watched her, amused. He didn't even seem much concerned about her announcement.

"That's not like you, to hang on to one of them. You'll find someone else. The sky's the limit, baby."

"Spare me the platitudes," she seethed.

"Okay then," he said, his tone so serious all of a sudden, it made Grace flinch. When Edward talked in this tone, he meant business and accepted no messing around. "You can't stay here. We can't stay here. You know damn well why."

"Do I? Everything is fine. I read the newspaper this morning."

"And that's all the proof you need," he said sarcastically.

"You're the one who wanted to lay down roots in your hometown."

Edward considered her words for a moment. "Actually, yes, you're right. I guess we're staying a little while longer, see how things pan out. Stay away from that girl though. I know her. You don't want that kind of attention."

Grace gave him a small smile and a nod.

"Did you hear what I just said?"

"Okay, okay." She threw her hands in the air. "I'm not going to call her anymore. She can't keep me from going to my favorite bar. I can easily find someone younger and prettier than her there."

"Then why didn't you do so in the first place?" Edward asked mildly.

Chapter Four

"What part of don't go near this case didn't you understand? This is so typical. Remind me to never trust you again. You are unbelievable!"

Joanna had hoped she'd have a little more time until Theo returned. It turned out she wasn't that lucky.

"Um...maybe we should take this outside?" she ventured.

"No. This is okay. I'd like Joanna to stay," Christina said. "Detective, there's something I have to tell you."

"Ms. Danvers, if this woman bothered you..."

"This woman is my friend."

Christina made a dismissive gesture when Theo gave her an incredulous look.

"I know about the Decker story," she said. "I can't say I'm worried about this now. The man who abducted me has killed before, as it seems, and he's still out there. That scares me senseless."

"Believe me, we're doing everything we can...Why didn't you mention you knew each other?" he asked suspiciously. There was a tense silence before both women realized the question had been for Joanna.

"That's because we didn't. I make friends quickly."

"I'm not naïve," Christina added. "She's the first person who makes me think someone could find him."

Joanna winced.

"Well, then, thanks J, for instilling so much confidence in regular police work. Ms. Danvers, what is it you remember?"

Christina sent Joanna an imploring look, and she answered for her.

"The guy was with his girlfriend, and they invited her to what they said was a kinky sex party. In the motel, it was just the three of them, though. There was consensual sex at first, but then they had drinks, and Christina remembers very little after that. I'm thinking GHB."

"A kinky sex party," Theo repeated, looking confused.

"Don't you understand? Christina, we're going to step outside for a moment, okay?" Outside the room, she continued, "The slasher is moving up in the world. Instead of using pencils to stab away, he's planning, drawing lines on the women's bodies, cutting patterns. And he's gone from simple hook-ups to sex parties. Well, those might not actually exist, but there is someone helping him, a woman! It's harder to remain unseen if they work as a couple!"

Her cheeks were flushed. Joanna had almost forgotten that there had been years of prison and the traumatic ending of a case in between the present and the last time she'd tried piecing together clues leading to a murderer. It wasn't something she could simply turn off.

"Yeah, well, thanks. That's all helpful and we'll take everything into consideration. Still, it's my ass on the line every time you pull a stunt like this, and I'm not going to stand for it. Believe me, no one in the department is going to stand for it either, so stop it."

The cease-fire was over.

"Don't worry. That's all I got."

"Just like that?"

"I swear," Joanna said. "I wanted to make sure you got the slasher connection, and I had a hunch about something missing from her statement. Did you find the place where she ran from yet?"

"Wait a minute. You didn't even see her statement," Theo said incredulously. "Or...did you? Did Vanessa...?"

"No, she's innocent in all of this. Speaking of which...you guys better be careful. You are not good for each other's careers."

"What is that supposed to mean?"

"You know exactly what it means. Don't mess with her."

Theo sighed. "I didn't plan to. As long as we both do our jobs, there's no conflict of interest here, or whatever it is you're alleging. Can I at least count on you to keep your mouth shut?"

"Why wouldn't I? Gossip was never my strong suit, even when I still had a job at the department."

"Was it worth all of that? Losing everything?" His anger had vanished. Joanna told herself it would be wise to leave it at that.

"I never looked at it that way. I didn't feel like I had a choice."

"You should have gone with temporary insanity. A few therapy sessions instead of jail time."

"And then what? No, it was better that way. I paid my dues to society, or whatever. Can I go now? I have to go to work."

"You could do other work than that." Apparently, Theo knew what she was doing. Joanna wondered if she had been a subject of conversations between him and Vanessa.

"It was tough enough to find that job. Look, I'm sorry for messing with your case, but I thought—no, I know—these are important elements. I don't want a pat on the shoulder. I just want someone to catch this asshole, doesn't matter if it's not me."

"All right. Thank you."

"You're welcome. See you around."

Another shift passed by with her concentration waning. This time, it was Joanna who had left out one detail, and it kept bothering her. Was Grace's outrageous suggestion a coincidence?

It couldn't be anything other than that, Joanna told herself. Otherwise, she had slept with, if not a murderer, then an accomplice to murder.

If she had told Theo to look into it, she would have to admit to the possibility. Joanna wasn't sure she could live with it, as the mere thought made her sick to her stomach. So much for responsibility, doing the right thing. Grace hadn't mentioned kinky sex parties, just a boyfriend. Joanna knew that these offers sometimes floated around in the scene, from straight women who were looking to experiment with their boyfriend's blessing. That didn't mean either of them was a killer. It didn't mean they weren't.

The slasher's type was younger than her, and a lot more put-together, someone like Christina.

She had been an investigator on his case though. He was bound to remember her.

If...

She couldn't take the risk.

Grace's last message said. *I'm sorry for bothering you. I don't know what I was thinking. You'll never hear from me again.*

She called Theo and laid out her dilemma.

"I don't think I'll ever understand you."

Joanna could sympathize. For the past few years, she had trouble understanding herself.

"I'll keep a low profile as promised. I just wasn't sure...It could be nothing."

"You were right to tell me," he said.

"Keep me up to date if anything comes up?"

Something must have tipped him off, told him that she was more shaken by the possibilities than she wanted to let on. The hands that had touched her might have killed. At the very least, they might have touched a killer, tainted her by proxy. After trying for years to escape the bone-chilling darkness men like the slasher and Decker had cast on her life, this was not welcome.

Nowhere was safe.

"You're going to be okay," he said.

Joanna laughed wryly. "The jury is still out on that, but I appreciate the vote of confidence."

∗

The next day, she ran into Nate who had come in to talk to the boss before he left on his vacation. She had made a promise to Theo...Then again, this was an opportunity impossible to miss. Just to check this one more item off the list.

"Nate, hi. Can I talk to you for a second?"

Joanna couldn't blame him for the suspicion in his gaze. She probably knew better than anyone else what he'd been through in the past days, the scrutiny and the suspicion. The only difference was that she was guilty, not just an innocent bystander.

"Yeah, so?" He knew who she was though they had never exchanged more than a few words.

"I work in the warehouse."

"I know. What do you want?"

"About Christina Danvers..."

"I don't want to talk about it anymore, okay? It was horrible. I'm glad she made it. Reporters have been camping out in our street and harassing my wife and kids. We're really due for a break."

"I understand that. I'd just like to know..." The problem was, Joanna wasn't even sure what she wanted to know from Nate. God, she'd become rusty. "When you found her, she was barefoot, dressed in only a sweater?"

"It's all in the newspaper."

"Nate, come on. I'm not sure if you know, but I used to be a cop. I need to...This sounds exactly like a case I worked on, and I need to find out if the two are connected. My old partner is aware that I'm asking a few questions." Sort of. "You drive that route often? Have you ever observed anything strange up there?"

"Good Lord, you're as bad as the rest of them. What the hell do you think I do when I'm on the job? I drive. I stop as often as I have to, not more. I did what I could to help her. That's all I can tell you. Can I get back to work now?"

Joanna wasn't done.

"How long do you think she could have made it, with barely any clothes on her? I saw her in the hospital. She can't have walked that long. The place where they took her, it had to have been somewhere close by."

"That's for the real police to find out, don't you think?"

She ignored the sting.

"Nate. You did a great job. She's alive because of you."

Nate turned away, but not before she'd seen the pain in his expression.

"I can't stop thinking about her. I'm not sure a vacation is going to change that, and I hate letting down my family, because they wished for this for so long. They deserve to have that time, but I...I keep seeing her face everywhere," he choked out.

"I know how you feel, I really do," Joanna said softly. "Most of the ones I saw, didn't make it, though. Every little detail can help. If you remember anything..."

"I'll call the cops first. Thanks for reminding me."

"Okay. You try to relax a bit on that vacation. I know it's hard, but you earned it too."

"Thanks," he said. "I told this to the police already, but there's not much on this stretch of road. A handful of residential buildings. It happened right after a diner I had stopped once before. I'm sure they asked everyone already."

"Yeah, they would do that. Thank you, Nate. I have to go back to work too."

Joanna did, but her mind was on Christina Danvers running away from the killers, barefoot and wounded, in a snowstorm. She was extremely lucky to have run into Nate. The place where she'd been held couldn't have been far, yet it seemed like the police hadn't found it yet.

Unless...they hadn't released that information for a reason.

After her shift, she drove out of the city and toward the area where Nate had found Danvers. Like he'd described, houses were sparse alongside the road. Joanna saw a gas station and a few miles further, a sign for a rest stop. It wouldn't be uncommon for the slasher to hide out in the woods, but he would need supplies.

Most of the houses here belonged to families who had lived in the area for a long time, some had vacation rentals. They would be aware of anyone out of place...but maybe he wasn't.

Joanna remembered Decker's neighbors, in complete shock when they realized what he'd done. Never raised his voice, always so polite. He had lived in the neighborhood for thirteen years. His basement was sound-proofed, and there was a room his wife had never set foot in.

Alarmed by the possibility of having a real flashback while driving on this lonely road, Joanna located the diner Nate had mentioned, ready to counter the sickening images with some hearty food.

When she walked in, she noticed the uniformed cops in one booth, one local, two State Police. This was...interesting. Their table was empty, no sign that they had even ordered yet. She'd hang out here a little longer, see if there was something she could take away.

And what if? Would seeing the place where Christina was held make a difference? She wasn't psychic, didn't have flashes of the perpetrator while at a crime scene. It was all about the hard work of many individuals brought together, and even then, it sometimes amounted to very little.

That man was still out there, with his girlfriend. Possibly Grace. Was it really that obvious, or was she becoming paranoid, falling for an outlandish conspiracy theory?

The cops in the booth conversed quietly, too quietly for her to overhear.

They were taking a break, so it didn't seem like there was anything acutely happening, but for sure, they had a reason to be around here. Joanna ordered a burger and fries and sat down at the counter. One of the men got a phone call, and they all got ready to leave, prompting her to take her order to go.

She followed the two cars at a distance—they were professionals, after all—asking herself once again what the hell she was doing. Or maybe that was Theo's voice in her head.

What if she could help? She had spent many hours, then days and weeks on the slasher case, trying to put together the pieces, the spree from California, across the country, to his current location. He came back, why? To mess with the investigators, with her? How did Grace fit into all of this? Was meeting her at The Copper Door more than a coincidence? He might know Joanna got out of prison.

When the cars slowed down, she drove past and parked a block away. From there she could see the road they had taken up to a wooded area with few cabins and vacation homes.

Joanna waited.

She'd stay here until they came back, and take a look for herself, just from afar, nothing to mess with the crime scene. It was probably crazy. She could be in her apartment, have a drink, relax. The problem was Joanna hadn't relaxed much in the past years, and she wasn't sure she knew how to. She picked up a pack of cigarettes, then reconsidered and ate her food instead. It was lukewarm, but at the moment it was the only comfort she could get.

It took about half an hour for the cars to return. Joanna concluded nothing major had happened. When the taillights disappeared in the distance, she took the same road off the highway and into the woods.

The slasher never killed his victims at the same site. He preferred dark remote places—somewhere to scuttle about like the roach he was. When she got out of the car, she saw the yellow tape right away. It was going to snow tonight, so she wouldn't have to worry too much about tracks.

Remote houses, bloodied bodies and traces of ball pens and markers in the wounds. Her stomach churned violently. Joanna thought with regret that all the past years had done was to make her more vulnerable. She used to be able to live with the sights and sensations, believing she could actually make a difference.

"You can't stay away, can you?"

She flinched at the sound of Theo's voice. "I should have expected you to be here."

"You are lucky that I know you. Otherwise, I would be concerned by your passionate interest in my crime scenes. What is it going to take, Joanna? When are you going to understand this is not your concern anymore?"

"You're the one who doesn't understand," she said, angry that he had caught her off guard. "I'm still a woman. It does concern me."

"Try to be fair for a moment, Joanna. Everyone's here is busting their asses to find him and Grace, men *and* women."

"So, she is a person of interest?" Joanna didn't know whether she should be excited or appalled.

"She is. Look, there are people who are working this case. Don't assume for a minute that they need you because they might not be skilled enough, or as determined as you are, because they are. You helped us, and I acknowledge that. What do you want? A prize?"

There was some truth to his words, Joanna had to admit. It didn't make her concerns any less real. "I never said that."

"Then why are you even here?"

"I need to see him go down," Joanna said quickly, before she had the chance to make a more shameful confession. She knew it would be saner to keep her distance. A sane person would take the chance to stay away from death and horror if they could. Yet, she had felt an urgency ever since Vanessa brought up the subject of the murders. "Okay, here it is. I'm terrified that we overlooked something back then, and that it could happen again, and it's my fault."

Theo shook his head. "No. There was nothing else you, or anyone else, could have done. Hell, the FBI didn't catch him. You have some serious issues to work on, but this case is in good hands. Let's leave it at that."

"You did contact the FBI to see what they had?"

"What do you think?"

"I'm sorry," she relented. Sighed. "I know you got it covered. Just let me know when you get him, okay?"

"I will. Now go home. It's freezing out here."

"I wonder if he used this site before."

"He never once used the same site."

"Yeah, but I'm not so sure anymore. It's remote, but this is close enough to the highway to get everything he needs...and he wouldn't need to stay up here for long. It might be worth it to open up the ground. He came back to the area after all. There's something, or someone, around here for him."

Theo looked thoughtful.

"I don't think so. They went to the motel, but didn't intend to kill her there, too messy. This house has been abandoned for a long time. The owner died, and there were no relatives. Our killer knows his way around here, how to get in and out quickly."

"It sucks that in this weather, traces don't stay. How does he get her out of the motel and up here, with no one noticing?"

"It's a motel. No one pays much attention in which condition people come in and out, sadly. We found some DNA up here though. And don't try to distract. We are both going home now."

"Yeah. I guess."

They parted ways, and Joanna drove straight home. She ran a hot bath to get warm and opened a bottle of beer. She couldn't remember buying the dark red bubble bath—a gift from someone, maybe? Kira?—but in the dimmed light, it looked like blood, making her shudder.

When would the memories stop? Would they ever? Joanna wondered if Nate was able to escape what he couldn't un-see during his Caribbean vacation. She doubted it, but it was nice to think of sun, beach, and the ocean.

Joanna was about to dispose of the printouts still scattered over her desk when her phone rang. She half feared it could be Grace again, half hoped Theo would get back to her with news, but of course it was too early for that. The connection was too vague for him to get a warrant, so he'd have to tread carefully.

Much to his credit, he hadn't commented on the fact that she couldn't give him a last name. There was no name on the door, and in her emails and text, it only said *GracieL*. Theo would have to do the rest, but she figured it wouldn't be too hard.

"Your apartment isn't that big," Kira said. "Why aren't you picking up the phone?"

Because I'm afraid it could be a serial murderer on the other end...

"Sorry," Joanna mumbled. "What can I do for you?"

"Call every once in a while? You're doing it again."

Kira had been the closest she'd had to a friend in prison, and surprisingly, she'd kept in touch, even after being released eight months earlier. Life could take surprising turns, and not all of them were bad, at least for people other than Joanna. Kira had found a kind man, the father of two boys, and married him less than two months ago. She often tried to convince Joanna to come to dinner, but Joanna wasn't comfortable around all that newfound happiness. Mostly, she thought her presence made others uncomfortable. Not Kira—she knew her friend understood completely what her reality looked like. The husband and kids, Joanna wasn't so sure. She felt like every time she was over, he was beyond wary.

"I'm not doing anything. In fact, you'll be glad to know that I reconnected with an old colleague."

"Vanessa doesn't count. You two have a sick relationship."

"Thank you so much, and no, I wasn't talking about Vanessa. I saw Theo, my old partner. He's talking to me again, which is a major improvement. Another officer let me talk to a witness once I laid on the charm."

"I don't understand. What are you doing with a witness? You unload trucks and lift palettes for a living—which, I'd like to say, is not such a bad thing. I thought that part of your life was over, and you were okay with it."

"It's a long story."

"You could come over and tell it to me."

"I don't think Coby would approve."

"Coby likes you," Kira protested. "Besides, he's not here tonight, and neither are the boys. I've got Merlot and chocolate chip ice cream. As much of it as you like."

"You're trying to bribe me?" Joanna didn't need much more. She was already in her coat.

"Works every time, doesn't it? I miss you."

"Miss you too. I'll be over there in ten."

Instead of staring at the walls, waiting for Theo's call and hoping her gut had betrayed her, she would see Kira, and toast to the future.

Yeah, right.

Sticking to her promise, Kira greeted Joanna with a hug and then served her ice cream and wine. It had become something like a ritual for them after Joanna's release, even after it became clear that Kira and Coby were serious, and they moved in together.

"This is so good. Thank you. I needed that."

"I'm glad I could help. You said you had a story to tell."

Joanna figured that halfway through her glass, she couldn't back out now.

"All right. You heard about the woman who ran away from a man who abducted her, and was found by a truck driver?"

"Yeah, I heard about it. What's that got to do with you?"

"I saw her in the hospital today."

"You did what?" Kira exclaimed. "Are you crazy?"

"The case is similar to one I once worked. I had to speak up."

47

"Going to the hospital is not the same. Honey, do you realize that any defense lawyer will just love to jump on the fact you were anywhere near her? You're famous. You killed a murderer. As unfair as that might be, I don't think your colleagues want to be seen with you, and sadly, they have a point. Someone will make the connection."

"Theo said something like that," Joanna admitted. "Damn, I had hoped for some support from you."

"This is the way I offer support," Kira indicated the delicacies on the table with a sweeping gesture, "and by telling you the truth. You can't be involved. I don't want you to put yourself in danger."

Joanna finished her glass and reached for the bottle.

"It might already be too late for that."

Before she could elaborate, the vibration of her cell phone indicated the arrival of a text message.

"Excuse me."

Once upon a time, she had known what to do, without hesitating, without doubt. After the brief conversation with Theo, Joanna felt confused. Relieved, too. Grace had apparently fully cooperated, told the cops she'd broken up with the boyfriend and apologized again for the text messages. More important, she had an alibi for the night Christina Danvers had hooked up with the couple.

Christina had confirmed that she'd never seen Grace before.

Something had been off about her. Joanna didn't think her instincts would betray her so badly. She shook herself. She should be grateful that she had avoided adding another nightmare to the ones that never went away.

"Are you okay?" Kira asked when she returned to the living room.

"Yeah. It's actually good news. Forget what I said earlier—it's not all that dramatic. All of you were right. I should stay far away from that case."

Kira poured them both another glass.

"Hey, better late than never. Let's drink to that. You should fall in love too."

"Uh, no. It's doesn't work that way for everyone."

"Because you have commitment issues. You panic when someone calls you back."

"That's not true." Was it? Was there a possibility that there was something wrong with Joanna instead of Grace? Oh, the possibilities were endless. "Look at my life. Who would want to get caught up in that mess?"

Kira laid an arm around her shoulders. "Last time I checked, you cleaned up that mess pretty nicely. Back on the inside, you could've gotten caught up in all kinds of bad stuff, but you stayed out of it. You have a job that pays for a roof over your head and more booze and cigarettes than you should have."

"I sense some criticism coming on."

"Just give it a chance sometime, won't you?"

Joanna took another spoonful of ice cream.

"I like fewer complications in my life. Simple pleasures, you know?"

"I really don't know. You hook up with some bizarre people. That's the only part you haven't quite figured out yet."

You don't know the half of it, Joanna wanted to say. Then again, she hadn't been so great at relationships before she and Decker crossed paths. For some things, she had no one to blame but herself.

"Maybe there's nothing to figure out. I get by."

And for a few hours, she'd been worried that her latest hook-up could have been a murderer's accomplice—or apprentice. Right, why change anything?

Chapter Five

F elicia felt like she was on top of the world. The fact that she'd almost had a bottle of wine by herself might have something to do with that, but she didn't care. She felt amazing. If only the jerk she'd dated for six months could see where she was now. What she could do.

She had noticed the new guy, Randy, in the club before. She'd been sure he was giving her the eye. Felicia decided that if he was there tonight, that would be it—and it got even better from there.

They had already made out in the corner booth of the club, and she was ready to go. He said he liked to draw it out, and that he had a surprise for her.

Felicity liked surprises, so she followed him back on the dance floor. He held her close, and a moment later, she was startled when someone came up behind her, embracing her from behind.

"I Ii," a soft voicc whispered. A woman's voice.

"You don't mind if Dana joins us?" Randy asked.

Felicia turned around, took a look at the woman and decided that no, she didn't mind. At this point, she was burning up with heat and imagination, and she couldn't wait to get somewhere more private with the two of them. The guy who left her last month?

She could barely remember his name.

"Not a problem," she said.

"Good. You won't regret it. Ready to go?"

If Felicia got any more ready, she'd commit indecent acts in public.

"There's a motel not far from here," Dana said. Her hand was on Felicia's hip, moving lower. Felicia wanted to moan. She barely kept in the sound.

"Relax, baby. It will be magical," Randy promised.

The motel wasn't anything luxurious, but Felicia didn't care. She barely noticed the trashy Christmas decoration near the entrance, or the man behind the counter whose grin said he knew exactly what was going on.

She soon forgot that the walls were probably paper thin, shivering in anticipation when Dana and Randy undressed her, and then each other. Felicia didn't hold back. It was the kind of place where no one blinked an eye when they heard moans and screams even. No room service, but the couple magically produced another bottle of wine, part of which ended up over Felicity's sweaty naked body.

She passed out.

❦

Before going out, Joanna made an effort to clean up her apartment, not that it took long. Kira's words remained with her, and she turned them over in her head, wondering what to do with them.

Not the falling in love part. Joanna was quite sure that it wasn't in store with her. She wanted to wash the taste of Grace, the bizarre memory, from her lips and mind, and she was hopeful she could find someone who'd help her with that.

She gathered the papers from her desk and, about to put them into the shredder, hesitated. There was no reason for her to keep them any longer. She had done her part.

Joanna picked up a folder instead, laid the printouts inside and put them into a drawer. It wasn't like she'd forget or could pretend this mess didn't exist.

She had made progress, Kira was right. The most important thing was not to blow it—or keep wondering how her life could have turned out, if she'd caught the slasher, if she'd made different choices.

It was Saturday night. She had earned a little fun.

To her relief, Grace was nowhere to be seen at The Copper Door. Vanessa sat at the bar, sipping her Martini.

"Uh-oh." Joanna slipped onto the barstool next to hers. "What's wrong?"

Vanessa grimaced. "Nothing much, except that I can't be seen in public with my boyfriend."

Joanna winced on her behalf. "Theo said that?"

"Not in so many words, but it's clear that he prefers to keep this our dirty little secret. In bed with IAB. Someone might take offense."

"It's not always easy to keep emotions out of the job." That hadn't been the right answer, or the one Vanessa wanted, Joanna could tell right away.

"You would know."

"Well, actually I would, and it cost me, as *you* know."

"That's not the same. I resent the idea that I can't have a love life and do my job. It's such a cliché that women can't do that."

"Is that really the problem here?"

Vanessa sighed. "Hell if I know. Relationships don't work. It's just too much investment with little to no return."

It sounded exactly like what Joanna had told Kira last night, yet she felt like she should protest.

"Don't tell me that isn't your premise. I know you messed around with anger issues girl."

It was Joanna's turn to sigh. "You know, I wish you two would talk about someone other than me every once in a while."

"Me too," Vanessa said. "But where you are concerned, we all have dues to pay. That, and your story never ceases to intrigue us."

"I'm not sure what to say to that."

When the bartender brought another Martini for Vanessa, Joanna ordered a red wine. Not something The Copper Door was famous for, but it was decent. She didn't want to start with the vodka, in case Vanessa's mood worsened, or that one true love for Joanna walked through the door.

Right. Number one was more of a possibility.

"You know why I did it, right?"

Here we go. "Of course," Joanna assured her. "We've been over this."

"I wanted the bastard dead just as much as you did. The difference between the two of us is that you picked up a gun and shot him four times."

Faith Rickers, Danielle Montgomery...

"The system doesn't work that way, and for a reason. If we all acted like that, there'd be chaos. Before I joined Internal Affairs, I saw enough kids accidentally shooting their friends or grandparents. We don't need vigilantes on top of that. Can you imagine how many people would get it wrong?"

"I didn't get it wrong," Joanna reminded her, wondering if they'd ever find it in themselves to let go of this subject.

"No, but he got off easy anyway. That kind of death was too good for him."

"I agree with you on that. Every time that happens, we should have another drink."

"No, let's have a drink every time we *don't* agree," Vanessa said. "Otherwise, I'll never get a proper buzz going. What about you? You want to take someone home tonight?"

"Slow down. I've been here for fifteen minutes."

"That's usually your speed. What are you waiting for?"

As if on cue, a woman walked inside, clutching her purse to her chest as if she was worried someone might steal it. She was wearing a knee-length burgundy coat and black high-heeled boots. No hat. Her hair was damp with melting snowflakes.

Joanna realized she had watched for a little too long when the woman caught her gaze and quickly looked away.

Vanessa had missed the subtle interaction, and Joanna directed her attention back to her. "Don't worry about me. If you want to talk..."

"We've already talked more than I intended. Let's drink some more."

It occurred to Joanna that all of her friends, her included, had similar coping strategies. Of course, Kira was the one who got the jackpot, but she, too, had a past she was trying to run from. Would any of them ever completely succeed? Joanna doubted it.

"I'm with you on that. Let's forget about all the people that complicate our lives for a while."

Something, however, made her sip her wine slowly, and she kept stealing glances at the woman sitting at the other end of the bar and checking her phone every once in a while. She was probably waiting for someone, Joanna reasoned. Forty-five minutes later, and judging from the woman's frustrated expression, it was likely that he or she had stood her up. It was enough time for Joanna to come up with alternate scenarios in her mind.

Some sexy. Some disturbing. She remembered what Christina had told her about finding the couple in the bar. Random encounters came with a risk, always. She tried to concentrate on the brighter options.

"What do you want from life?" Vanessa asked, blitzed enough to become philosophical. "I mean, this uphill battle thing we're doing, it can't be all, right? Do your job, or do what's right, and you always get screwed over anyway for the lack of a dick."

Joanna almost choked on her sip of wine, but she couldn't help laughing. There was a reason why she actually *liked* hanging out with Vanessa.

The woman gave her a hesitant smile. She was beautiful, probably a neat person judging from her getup, kind, nice to strangers. The kind of person a predator would go for.

"Right now? I want her."

"Yeah, and I want a promotion," Vanessa said, slurring her words slightly. "Let's see which one of us gets a reality check first."

"Hey. I'm good at this. Watch me."

Vanessa turned on her barstool.

"I dare you. Fifty bucks if you go home with her."

"Fifty bucks? You're not only depressed, you're cheap tonight."

"Okay, a hundred," Vanessa grumbled.

Joanna chuckled.

"I could use it, but you didn't think I was that bad, right? This kind of thing is so frat boys. We're above that, right?"

Barely, but still.

"She's way too high maintenance for you."

"She's too high maintenance for this place, but so are you, and yet you keep coming back. Now pay attention. I'm sure you can learn something."

The woman was drinking white wine, and before Joanna got up to join her on the other end of the bar, she asked the waiter to bring her another glass. The woman looked surprised, but she smiled politely when she realized who had paid for her drink.

"I'm not sure what this is for, but I can use it. Thanks."

"You're welcome. You're alone here?"

"Looks like it. You're not."

"She's my straight best friend. We all got one of those, don't we? Okay, now, that was stupid. It's true though that she's a friend, and she's definitely straight. Can we start over? I'm Joanna."

"Rue. Nice to meet you, Joanna." She laid her hand into Joanna's, the gesture a lot more sensual and promising than a normal handshake.

"Likewise. So, were you meeting someone here? They must be stupid to stand you up."

"That's what I keep telling myself. That, and no more online dating. Ever."

"That's wise. There are some crazy individuals out there."

"Speaking from experience?" Rue asked. She seemed interested. Joanna thought that she might have to call a cab for Vanessa, should this go anywhere.

"I've got experience. You want to know more about that?"

Rue laughed. "All right, I think that must have been one of the worst lines I've ever heard but go on. I'm intrigued." A moment later, she added, sounding worried, "Ouch, that didn't come out too bitchy, did it?"

"No. I think I deserved it. I never tried online dating, by the way. I did meet some crazy people though."

"What do you do?"

"Currently, I load trucks." She shrugged at Rue's surprised expression. "I used to be a cop, in Homicide."

There was actually a person in this town who had never heard about her story. Amazing.

"That must have been tough. What happened?" Rue blushed. "I'm sorry, I didn't mean to be nosy."

"That's okay. It didn't work out for me, and besides, I sat behind a desk for a lot of the time. Now is not so bad, actually. I enjoy the physical work."

"I can imagine." Rue looked her up and down, and this time, she didn't blush.

It was Joanna instead who felt the rush of heat in sensitive places. She reached for her glass. "What about you?"

"Oh, it's not that interesting. I'm a personal assistant to a CEO, and I think I'm stuck there for the rest of my career. He's a pretty conservative guy, doesn't really see much of a leadership potential in women."

"That's too bad. I'm sure you're good at taking the lead."

"I'm flexible," Rue said, her gaze lingering. She shook her head. "Now listen to me, I have no idea where that came from. I'm sorry. All of a sudden, I'm kind of nervous."

"Why?" Joanna hoped she was at least partly responsible. The more time she spent in Rue's presence, the more she felt optimistic she could be The One. Not what Kira had in mind, of course, just to take her mind off Christina, the slasher, and the memory of her disastrous encounter with Grace. Come to think of it, that was a lot to expect of someone.

"I wonder where you think this is going."

"Do you want it to go anywhere? I'm flexible too, you know."

"I'm glad. Would you think I'm a slut if I invited you to my place tonight?"

There was no way in hell Joanna would think that. First of all, she had no talking room at all, and second, she was already imagining them together, naked.

"Hell, no. I love the idea."

"I can't, though," Rue said with honest regret. "I'm not going to lie, I had forgotten about this douche from the Internet

58

the moment I saw you. I was pretty sure you were with your friend over there, but since you aren't...I kind of feel the need to slow down. I mean, would you even be interested to have dinner, a real date? I don't do one-night stands, at least I haven't so far, and this is...I'm not making any sense, am I?"

"You are. I understand."

"Or maybe I blew it, and I'll never see you again."

"Not going to happen," Joanna promised. "I'm pretty easy to find. The drunk lady over there and I are here all the time." The problem was, in the meantime, Rue could find out the truth. What was happening anyway, seeing the same woman twice, again? That had not been the plan.

"That's a relief. I'd like to get to know you a little bit before...You know."

Once again, Joanna thought of Christina.

"Smart of you. For all you know, I could be into all kinds of kink, and then we'd have to make sure we are on the same page." What she really wanted to say was, *smart of you, because there are some sick people out there, like serial killers*. That was the reality.

She still wanted to make the best out of this unexpected, so far pleasant situation. She had to live sometime.

"So, are you? Into kink?"

"Not really. I hope that doesn't disappoint you."

"It doesn't. I have plenty of other ideas."

"I look forward to hearing about them."

They were both lost in the fantasy for a moment before Vanessa joined them, breaking the spell.

"Hey, J, I just wanted to say I'm leaving. Theo is going to pick me up. Good night..."

"Rue," Rue supplied helpfully, shaking hands with Vanessa.

"Cool. See you around." She winked at Joanna and left.

"She's not normally like that," Joanna said.

Theo arrived minutes later, and Joanna saw Vanessa get into his car.

"Where were we...sexy ideas?"

Rue laughed. "Thank you. This is the most normal conversation I've had in a while."

"The online stuff must be really bad, then."

"Worse than you can imagine."

Actually, Joanna could imagine, because Decker had found some of his victims online. What would it take to stop thinking about him? Or the man who had taken Christina Danvers?

She had to admit though that Rue put her at ease in a way she hadn't expected. The problem with rushed, casual encounters was that there was only a small window, someone was always in a hurry. For the first time in a long time, words mattered.

"That doesn't make me want to try, honestly. So, tell me more about you. Why do you work for that boss who stymies your career? I'm sure you could do a lot better."

"Maybe. Probably. It's just hard to make that kind of change when you have a sure paycheck coming in each month."

It wasn't exactly the same, but Joanna could relate. After a few months at the warehouse, she wasn't much motivated to move up in the world. The lulling effect of dubious security.

Rue shrugged. "The Christmas bonus wasn't so bad. For now, I can live with the rest. I know, that's bad. Principles and all. I try to make up for it by giving to Planned Parenthood."

"That's more than most people do. And following your principles can get you into trouble sometimes. What would you say if we went somewhere else? Would you like to go dancing?" It was hard to tell who was more surprised by the suggestion. "If I don't seem the type, you're kind of right. I haven't done that in forever, but since we're not...I think it would be a nice way to top off the night, don't you think?"

"I'd love to."

Joanna picked up Rue's coat and held it up for her to slip into it, a gesture that was appreciated, she could tell from Rue's small, contented smile. Joanna would have liked to get her out of her clothes rather than into them, but she sensed that this time, patience was a virtue that would pay off. Standing this close, she got a whiff of Rue's perfume, a light flowery scent. She wanted to lift those soft wavy strands and press her lips against her neck. Maybe on the second date. Maybe later. She wanted to go to a place that didn't come with twenty-somethings jumping up and down, or worse, teens who got in with a false ID.

She was looking for more of a classy place, somewhere she could look, perhaps touch, fireworks to come later. At this point, it was pretty clear that there would be fireworks—and her instincts hadn't been so wrong. She should have never hooked up with Grace. There was something strange about her, even if it wasn't "murder accomplice" strange.

Being with Rue made the difference all the more obvious.

"You have a place in mind?" Rue asked.

"Yes. Trust me?"

"I think we've already established that I do."

"Good. It's not too far from here."

Outside, the sidewalk had transformed into something close to an ice rink. Joanna hadn't lied, the club she had in mind wasn't far, but with the snow and ice, they spent more time sliding than walking. Rue giggled when Joanna stopped her from slipping on her high-heeled boots once more.

"Not far from here is a very relative term."

"It wasn't like that earlier," Joanna defended herself. "Would you like me to call a cab? It's just one more block, though."

"I'm fine," Rue said, her breath warm against Joanna's cheek.

Even out here in the cold, the warmth spread to other places quickly. Depending on when that second date would happen, she saw a lot of cold showers in her future.

"Good. I've got you."

"Lucky me."

That was debatable, but for one night, Joanna wouldn't question her own luck too much. They reached the club and stepped inside, and just like Joanna remembered, the décor and music was classic and understated, a lot quieter than The Copper Door. If she had known she'd come here tonight, she would have dressed up a little more. She hoped Rue would fulfill the casual chic dress code for both of them.

On the dance floor, she pulled Rue close to her, meeting no resistance. While The Copper Door was more in her price range, she enjoyed the laid-back atmosphere and even more, the woman who fit so comfortably into her arms. It was a bit confusing, to say the least, the mix of warmth and comfort with the heat and promise of sex that would hopefully live up to her imagination this time.

Maybe that was part of the problem, that lately there had been no room for imagination, just a simple social contract that left her empty every time.

Joanna still believed every word she'd told Kira. That didn't mean she couldn't delve into this world every once in a while, get to know a person beyond what they liked in bed. Not that she wasn't eager to find out everything Rue liked in bed and then make sure it happened. Rue leaned into her with a happy sigh, the closeness igniting her further. She hoped Rue felt the same, that she was at least a little impatient for the moment to arrive.

"Where have you been the past few months?" Rue murmured. "I can't believe I've been wasting so much time with weird folks on the Internet when I could have had this."

"I can be weird, but...thanks. I'll take it as a compliment."

"As you should."

The song was coming to an end. Rue showed no signs of wanting to stop, so they danced for several more.

"I don't want to go home yet, but I need a break. I feel like champagne. I'll buy."

Joanna's doubts must have shown on her face, because Rue was quick to add, "You paid for my wine, remember? No matter how far this is going, I prefer things to be equal. Just because I let you hold the door open for me once, it doesn't mean you have to pay for everything. Are you okay with that?"

"Sure. Just be warned the prices aren't exactly the same."

Rue laughed as she took Joanna's hand and led her off the dance floor.

"You know, when my date first suggested The Copper Door, I was kind of scared. I'm so happy I went. Come on."

How could Joanna say no to her?

She still cringed at the price of the champagne—not sparkling wine—but Rue handed her credit card to the waiter without blinking. If she wasn't completely delusional, Joanna would have a chance to repay her sometime, if not tonight. She was a decent cook when she put some effort into it. She was more than decent at other things. She couldn't wait to show Rue, who had been scared to set foot in The Copper Door but had done so anyway and thought the fact that Joanna had made a move was champagne-worthy.

Most of all, it felt good to be close to her, so in the private booth, after taking a sip of her drink—the good stuff—Joanna leaned close to kiss her. They'd go separate ways later tonight, but there were no restrictions on kissing, she learned when Rue's lips opened to her eagerly. She pulled her closer. Minutes passed before they leaned back. There was a soft blush to Rue's cheeks, her eyes sparkling.

Joanna didn't mean to change her mind, just give her a preview of what was waiting for her.

"You know what they say about instant gratification, and that it's more mature not to give in to it." Rue laughed, a bit breathless.

"Yeah. Apparently, anticipation makes it all better."

"You know what?" Rue reached out to trace a finger over Joanna's lips, the gesture making her shiver. "I think I've had enough anticipation. Would it bother you if I changed my mind?"

"No. Not at all."

"We still can't go to my place though. I'm in the middle of a bathroom renovation, and it's a construction site out there."

Joanna thought of her apartment and the fact that she hadn't welcomed anyone there in some time. She didn't mind a tad messy, but she didn't know that the same went for Rue. She wanted something better, less distracting for Rue.

"There's a hotel just one block down the street. I'll pay."

If Rue was disappointed Joanna didn't invite her into her home, she didn't let it show.

"That's a good idea. I don't want to wait any longer."

The relief Joanna felt came from many different reasons. Regardless of whether they'd have the second date or not, this sort of beginning set the parameters for their relationship, and she was just fine with that. Kira was still wrong.

Even better, she and Rue were on the same page—no need to repeat the disaster she'd had with Grace. This time would be different.

Chapter Six

Within seconds of closing the door of the hotel room, shoes were off and coats on the floor, no need to pretend any longer. Stepping behind Rue, Joanna brushed her hair aside to kiss her neck, her hands wandering to explore her body. Rue gasped, leaning back against her, giving her all the access she wanted.

Joanna ran her hands over Rue's legs, up to the hem of her dress and underneath. She slipped her fingers beneath the waistband of her pantyhose, and then inside her panties, feeling her warm and aroused.

"And you wanted to wait until next week?"

"Silly. I know."

"Did you imagine you were going to a hotel room with that date?"

"Not a chance. I don't think they'd be as good...oh. Wait," Rue said, the word a direct contradiction to her lustful tone, but even so, Joanna obliged.

Rue turned around. "I want to see you," she said. "I also want to get horizontal for this. I can have a little patience—when I know it's worth it."

"Okay."

Under her gaze, Joanna undressed, something she found strangely erotic. Usually it was her taking control, being the last one to take off her clothes. Rue had hinted earlier that she liked to lead on occasion, and Joanna wasn't opposed to the idea, on the contrary. Rue pulled her dress over her head and took off her stockings.

"You're sure you didn't plan on getting naked with someone tonight?"

The lingerie in different shades of blue suggested otherwise to Joanna, not that it should have mattered at the moment.

"I swear. I thought I'd be more confident for some reason. I'm not sure that worked, but now I'm glad for the foresight. Come."

"That's pretty much unavoidable sometime soon," Joanna said dryly. Rue laughed, reaching out her hand.

She let herself be drawn onto the bed, into her embrace, finally skin to skin, the heat building. Then she was on her back, Rue on top of her, kissing her deeply. Joanna leaned back into the pillow, happy to let go and let herself be ravished by a curious mouth. Anticipation was great when you knew where it was leading.

Joanna held on to the pillow under her head in a white-knuckled grip, red-hot pleasure igniting her body. For all her talk about ideas she'd had for this moment, she was ready to submit and let Rue have all the control, if only for the moment.

The rush of heat was incredible. What an amazing difference, she reflected, between doing this with someone you had some sort of connection with. Not the kind Kira was thinking about, no way, but there was something to be said about chemistry.

"Relax," Rue whispered. "It's Saturday night. We have time."

Joanna wondered if there was enough time to do everything she wanted to do to her. There was only one way to find out.

Joanna hadn't slept so deeply in many days. When her cell phone rang, she felt disoriented as to place and time for a moment. She cast a fond look over at Rue who was blinking sleepily, the sheet not covering all of her. They had fallen asleep from sheer exhaustion, the way it should be when all the elements were in place.

For the first time in a long time, Joanna didn't feel hung over either. She couldn't wait to have a hearty breakfast. Maybe Rue would like to join her. It was Sunday after all.

"It's early," Rue said, matter-of-factly, and it wasn't until then that the time registered with Joanna: 4.25 a.m.

"Hello? Who is this?"

"Thank God! Joanna, I need you to come here now."

"Who—?" It dawned on her before she could finish the sentence. "Christina?"

There was a flash of...something in Rue's expression, gone too quickly to determine. Irritation? Jealousy?

"Where are you?"

"Still in the hospital. The police were here." Christina was crying. "Another woman was murdered."

"What?"

"You said you were my friend. I'm scared. I did something for you, so could you come?"

"Of course. I'll be there in twenty minutes."

This time, she couldn't have missed Rue's reaction. She pulled up the sheet and turned away.

"Look, this is so not what you think it is. I went to see her a few days ago. You might have seen her story on the news. She got away from her kidnapper."

"I thought you said you were not a cop anymore."

"I'm not. The truck driver who saved her, he's a colleague of mine. I swear it's the truth." For some reason, she was desperate to make Rue believe her. "I met her recently, and she's having a really bad time as you can imagine. I told her she could call me."

"At four in the morning?" Rue still sounded somewhat dubious, but at least she was facing Joanna.

"Something came up. Please, sleep a little longer and meet me for breakfast downstairs at ten? I'll explain everything, I swear."

Rue regarded her thoughtfully. "This is not your backup, get out of jail free card? No ex or BFF trying to spare you the even more awkward conversation?"

"I promise you, that's not the case." Joanna couldn't help wincing at the metaphor, but as to Rue's worries, she had a clean conscience. "See you later?"

She leaned over to kiss her, and to her relief, Rue didn't pull away.

Another woman. Joanna would never admit it out loud, but she was almost as scared as Christina.

It wasn't over.

❧

The receptionist had a radio playing Christmas music on low. In the early morning hours, the hospital seemed almost peaceful, except everyone's peace had been rudely interrupted.

"Thank you for coming. I didn't know who to call."

"That's all right."

Joanna could sympathize even without a lengthy explanation from the distraught woman. Not everyone could understand hell, and unless they didn't have to, most people preferred not to take a closer look. Neither Christina nor Joanna could turn away. They had seen it up close.

"The police, what did they tell you?"

"They asked me again about the woman, but I swear, I told them everything now. The woman I saw was blonde, blue eyes.

Apparently, they have a witness who saw them leaving, and the description doesn't match. She could have colored her hair, right? They're not thinking that there's more than one couple out there that…"

"Kills? No, I don't assume they're thinking that. Look, I know you told the police everything already, but if you could help me out one more time…"

"What's in it for you? Why are you interested in this?" Christina shuddered. "If I were you, I'd be happy to be far away from all the madness."

"They're still out there," Joanna pointed out. "That's reason enough for me." That was why she had left a warm bed this morning after a promising night. She hoped Rue believed her and would wait for breakfast. She wanted to see her again, if only to repeat an experience that had, for a few hours, broken the circle of the ever-present question where she had gone wrong.

Not catching Decker soon enough. Not catching the slasher eleven years ago. All her successes seemed to pale in comparison, because she had done something to disqualify herself. Vanessa, Kira, Theo, even Christina, all her relationships were defined by the mistakes she'd made.

Not Rue.

The night with Rue had been far from a mistake. Joanna suppressed the impulse to smile. It would hardly be appropriate in a room with a woman who had barely escaped a serial killer and wasn't completely out of danger. Theo seemed to think the same thing, because he still had an officer assigned to guard her.

They always came back.

"You know, I never put anyone at risk intentionally." With the fear, there came anger. "I know there are already people alleging I deserved this, because what business did I have hooking up with a guy and his girlfriend? But these things happen all the time, everyone's on the same page, and no one's hurting each other. Then it's nobody's business. They...they tricked me, made me think I was safe with them. Until I woke up in that place."

"You were drugged. That's messing with your memory."

"No one knows how they got away so quickly."

"They probably came prepared, with a bigger vehicle, or a trailer."

The snow had been wet, mixed with rain. Every trace of the vehicles could have been washed away. This theory could explain though why the slasher cases had spread coast to coast, if he, if the couple had opportunity to pack up and leave whenever the trail got too hot—but how come no one had ever stopped them? They needed supplies, possibly weapons, tools to alter their appearance.

"I think you're right!" Christina sat up in her bed, a determined gleam in her eyes. "I got so dizzy and sick, felt like the ground was moving, but I thought it was the drugs. I'm trying so hard...I'm trying to remember how I got away, but all I can think of is running in the snow and falling down all the time. I don't think I even looked back once."

Frustration had won over hope once again.

"It's a good thing you didn't look back," Joanna assured her. "In the movies they always do, and that never ends well. I'll call Theo and see if that helps him in any way. They'll be on the lookout for a bigger vehicle, something big enough to hide the murder freak show."

"Okay. Thank you."

"No problem. Just for the record, I'll be glad to be far from the madness soon. I just want them caught, so this can be over."

"I appreciate it," Christina said.

On the way back to the hotel, Joanna called Theo. "You probably already know I saw Christina. Don't get mad—she called me. You scared her. She thinks she might have been in a moving vehicle, something like a trailer? Okay, who's that woman, and how reliable is the witness description?"

"No and no," Theo said. "It's nice talking to you again, and I'm sorry we all sucked as friends, but you promised."

"It's the slasher, right? Are you going to release a sketch to the press?"

"Whoa. Time-out. Joanna, am I speaking Chinese? Do my words make any sense to you at all?"

"Sorry," she mumbled.

"About that sketch. I need you to come in as soon as possible."

"What? I didn't do anything, I—"

"I know," he interrupted her. "Something came up. Not on the phone."

"Can I have breakfast first? There's somebody waiting for me."

"Tell her to wait a little while longer. I just need you to take a quick look."

"Can't you send it to me now? I swear I'll delete..."

The instant ping indicated a message sent. Joanna parked in the lot of the hotel and opened it.

"Oh my God. Damn. Fuck this."

"My sentiments exactly," Theo said dryly. "You really have a knack for attracting trouble."

Staring back at her from the sketch, hair straight instead of wavy, was Grace. Why hadn't Christina recognized her? She gave herself the answer. Hair color, make-up, and Christina had admitted she'd already had a few drinks by the time she met the couple. Joanna stared at the screen for a long moment, considering her options. She could make a positive ID and then leave it up to the professionals, that exclusive group she didn't belong to anymore. She could go back up, hide under the covers in the warmth of Rue's embrace and pretend she'd never been so desperate for sex and escape that she'd hooked up with a murderer.

Or she could do the right thing.

"It's her," she said. "Grace. I'm sure they use contact lenses in different shades, change hair color a lot. Can you meet me at the station? I just have to make a quick call. See you there."

Joanna realized she wasn't so brave after all.

I'm sorry, I won't be able to make it. Something came up, she texted.

There was no need to drag someone innocent into this mess.

Chapter Seven

I t was the first time Joanna had been to the department since her arrest. It was obvious that no one had forgotten, considering the heavy silence that fell over the room the moment she walked in. The place was busy. It might be Sunday, but with a new victim having turned up, there was no rest for the investigators. The killers were still in town. The police had to make sure they didn't get out.

Theo appeared out of nowhere, taking her arm.

"What do you think you're doing? Come with me."

When they were on the roof, out of the earshot of curious colleagues, he took out a pack of cigarettes and offered her one. Joanna gladly accepted. Act now, worry about the consequences later, as usual.

"Tell me about that other victim," she said.

Theo sighed. "Same MO. It's definitely them, and Grace, or whatever her name is, is part of this. By choice or coercion, we don't know yet. The apartment is empty, and the phone number she gave you doesn't exist anymore. We think he took her somewhere else, probably still within the city limits. We're keeping the idea of the trailer in mind."

She had assumed they were still around. Joanna wasn't so convinced of how Theo interpreted Grace's role in this mess.

"Come on. She seemed pretty independent to me."

"Looks can be deceiving. He probably watches her when she's approaching a victim...I'm sorry," he said when Joanna shuddered.

"Don't be. I think I was a distraction, nothing more. I don't fit the profile."

"You were an investigator on the case. Don't you think the slasher remembers you? Joanna, I want you to be more careful. Until we get this guy..."

"You want me to do what, take a vacation out of town? You seem to forget that I'm living on a different kind of paycheck now. Besides, Grace didn't contact me again. They killed another woman, and now they need to find a way to get out of town. So, tell me about her."

"The witness saw her dance with Grace. They seemed to spend most of the evening together, very hands-on. A man approached them, they talked for a few minutes and then all left together."

"She doesn't kill by herself," Joanna surmised. "Why do women trust men they don't know? Let me rephrase that. Why do women trust any men?"

"That's harsh."

"That's a valid question, actually. There aren't so many female serial killers."

"Except I have one on my hands now."

Joanna pushed her hands into the pockets of her coat.

"Look, I know you could get in trouble for discussing the case here with me. You got enough of that from our colleagues and the press after...Decker. I don't want that to happen again, but no one says we can't meet off the clock, at The Copper Door, or wherever we might run into each other. We could bounce off ideas. And...I'd like you to get me my old notes on the slasher. We need to compare past and present cases, see what changed besides Grace and the marker. We need a clearer profile. What happened? He hates women, yet he lets one work alongside him, to do what? Show off his power? Show Grace her place in the world?"

"You're the one who said she seemed independent," he reminded her.

That, in itself, was a victory. He hadn't brushed her off again. One foot in the door, one she wasn't sure she wanted to walk through, but didn't have a choice.

"Yeah. Maybe I should try to contact her."

"Are you out of your fucking mind? Okay, let me rephrase that. I thought you met someone."

"Gee, I need Vanessa to stay out of my affairs for five minutes or so."

He laughed. "Don't blame her. I saw you two together for five seconds, and that looked pretty intimate to me. Besides, you had to go somewhere earlier, so I thought..."

"You thought wrong. Who would want to get dragged into a disaster like this?"

"Come on..."

"The first time I called you after all this time, you yelled at me. Believe me, I know, being associated with me can kill your reputation. I have no illusions about that."

"You do have illusions about people's memory though. What happened was bad, there's no denying that. I can guarantee you most of the people downstairs dreamed about doing what you did, but there's a line that we draw, and if we step over it, we create chaos, not order."

"I know. I've had this conversation with Vanessa many times."

"Good, then it's about time you realize something. Even if you can't work for this department again and you made life difficult for quite a few of us..."

She shook her head and turned away. There was a killer couple on the loose, no time to turn this into a therapy session.

"It doesn't mean no one cares about you. Remember that sometime."

"Yeah, well, thanks. I need to..." Go to work, she'd almost said, but the truth was she had nowhere to go. Was her decision regarding Rue premature?

No, she decided. With the latest developments, it was even more important to keep her away, keep her safe. She'd always cherish the memory. Wasn't that one of those platitudes people used to console themselves?

When she was still working as a cop, with a reputation, a regular salary, and high hopes for her career, Joanna had been by the book. She used to shake her head about cop dramas and books in which the heroine went off by herself only for dramatic effect, to create the ultimate showdown.

She had become a fictional cliché, and it wasn't something she would recommend to anyone.

Back in her apartment, she went straight for the half-filled bottle of vodka, lighting another cigarette. Joanna wasn't sure if Theo would come through with her old files. It would be helpful to look at those notes now...She'd understand if he didn't. In the meantime, there was something she could do. He would be spitting mad and probably reconsider the cease-fire or giving a damn, but the results might be worth it.

The reason why Grace seemed so off and bizarre, might be that she was under some influence, drugs, intimidation, or both. If they could isolate her and convince her to give up the slasher...First, they had to find her. Joanna didn't owe anything to anyone. There was no book to go by anymore, and besides, no one could arrest her for asking questions.

She got up, picked up her keys and left, thought twice and went back to grab her coat when she saw the snowflakes swirling around.

Almost Christmas. For some reason, that made her think of Rue, something she had successfully avoided, and as if on cue, a missed voicemail popped up on her cell phone screen.

Hey, Rue said, *I'm really not into texting, sorry*. She laughed self-consciously, the sound filling Joanna with irrational longing. It had been just one night, damn it. She had other things to do now. Being distracted could get her killed...or worse, someone else. *I'm not sure I understand what's going on, but I'd love to see you again and just talk. Last night...It meant something to me. I hope you feel the same. See you soon and thanks for everything.*

She turned off the phone and walked the few blocks to The Copper Door, wincing at the Christmas music coming from the speakers. It was becoming infinitely harder to escape the holiday cheer. Luckily, she saw a familiar face behind the counter and approached the bartender.

"Hey. You remember the girl who kicked the jukebox?"

He filled a glass for her without asking. The gesture made Joanna cringe, but not enough to reject the offer.

"Yeah, the police were here to ask about her. You a cop?" She couldn't blame him for sounding this incredulous after seeing her come in night after night, drinking with Vanessa or by herself, and on occasion, hooking up with a woman.

"No. I was just wondering if you could help me find her. She left something of hers with me. If she comes in again, could you tell me? She has my number."

He mumbled something that sounded suspiciously like "I bet," then cleared his throat.

"Sure thing."

"Thanks." Joanna put a bill on the counter to pay for her drink, wondering what to do next. It was only early afternoon, and she didn't want to spend the day in here—she could sadly tell how that would work out.

She walked out at the same time another patron came in, and they nearly ran into each other.

"That's lucky," Rue said. "I was hoping I'd find you here."

Joanna didn't answer, feeling trapped in multiple ways besides the physical. She couldn't push her aside and leave, or run for the backdoor, both of which would make her look immature. She couldn't... "I'm sorry, I need to go."

"I think you owe me a word...some words. I'm sorry, that sounds bad. I don't mean to be that kind of woman, but I couldn't help feeling something changed after that phone call, and I'd like to know..." She took a deep breath. "Okay, please, let me start over. I haven't had breakfast yet. Could we go somewhere together? Just talk? I swear, if you want, I'll leave you alone after that. I just want to know where we're at."

Joanna wished she hadn't started the day on regrets and vodka. In the privacy of her apartment, it didn't matter if she was sorry for herself and giving in to the sentiment. Even though she was certain letting Rue go was the right choice, she didn't want to, and she felt deeply embarrassed by the present situation.

"I could use a coffee," she said.

"Good." Rue gave her a hopeful smile. "I'm starving. Last night was as exhausting as it was beautiful."

Joanna knew she was in deep trouble.

Rue had legitimate questions, she was sure, none of which Joanna could answer without telling her that only days before they met, she had hooked up with a murderer. She had overlooked signs, because usually it didn't matter, if you didn't plan on seeing the person ever again. It was what Joanna did. It might not be terribly healthy or sane, but getting close to someone, inevitably disappointing them, was worse, wasn't it?

To her surprise, Rue didn't press for answers. She seemed perfectly content to just sit in the café and chat. It had stopped snowing, and the clouds had moved to make room for a brilliant blue sky. More Christmas music. There was no escape.

"While I was trying to figure out what to do about your message, I did an internet search. I thought you looked familiar."

Here we go.

"Does that make me seem more interesting or insane?"

"You served your time. You don't owe me any explanation...for any of that, anyway."

"Maybe I do." Joanna held on to the cup like a lifeline. Maybe it was that she really wanted to touch Rue instead, believe that there was a way to outrun the shadows. "I don't have a definitive answer. I haven't thought about long term in...anything for quite some time, though I didn't lie when I said I wanted to see you again. There's just a lot of baggage I should have told you about sooner."

Rue shook her head. "I understand this isn't something you roll out on the first date, or even the morning after. Besides, everybody's got...stuff."

"Yep, you're working for the conservative guy. That's hardly a comparison."

"I never used to do one-night stands either or search my dates on the Internet. The truth is I want to spend more time with you, get to know you better, beyond what the newspapers said. If you want that."

"You're pretty brave."

"Selfish maybe. Last night...I loved every moment of it."

Me too. "It's not that easy. I'm kind of connected to this case now, and they haven't caught the killer yet. I don't want to..."

This sounded like a lame excuse even to Joanna, and she'd set the bar pretty low before.

"You think you're in danger? Or that I am?"

"I can't say for sure. That's enough to worry me."

"It's just that? Nothing I said or did?"

"Of course not. Everything you did was perfect."

Rue smiled as her cheeks reddened, and she took a hasty sip of her juice.

"Let's pretend for a moment all those complications didn't exist. What would you like to do with the rest of the day?"

There was no what if, when you were trying to make it day to day, paycheck to pay check—or when you had just put out the word for a likely dangerous individual to contact you.

Joanna knew for sure what she didn't want to do. Go home to her cold, lonely, not to mention, messy, apartment by herself. Do the sensible thing, or maybe irrationally feel responsible for every ugly thing in the world as usual. Theo was right—chances were Grace had long moved on.

Why couldn't she?

Joanna put a couple of bills on the table to cover the check and tip.

"Let's go," she said.

They walked along the river that was partially frozen, snow crunching under their boots. Rue linked her arm around Joanna's as they passed by a group of kids having a snowball fight.

When was the last time she'd gone out to simply take a walk that didn't lead her to The Copper Door or the next liquor store?

"I think we both need a change," Rue said. "Maybe we can inspire each other to get it done."

"You are surprisingly not freaked out. I don't know what to make of that," Joanna admitted.

"I think you and everyone else have been incredibly hard on you. I don't need to add to it. You crossed a line, and you paid for it. Maybe I need a little bit longer to process all of this, but it doesn't matter. What I *feel* is still the same. I felt safe with you."

"Thank you."

She hadn't even realized she'd said those words, not just in her mind, but in an urgent whisper.

❦

Felicity hadn't done the trick. Grace didn't understand why it was so easy for Edward to let go of Joanna when she couldn't. She had once hunted him, and from the looks of it, she was doing it again. Shouldn't that encourage him, challenge him? Even after working alongside of him for years, she hadn't completely figured him out, and it was driving her crazy. He was packing the van.

She stood, fists at her sides.

"Tell me again why we shouldn't have a go at her? We were careful. The police have nothing on us as long as we are careful about our appearances."

"You can't be careful enough," he said, unimpressed. "Besides, she doesn't interest me. Too old."

"Well, we all get older, even you, Prince Charming," she sneered, offended. The woman was younger than her, if only by a couple of years.

It was true that all of them had been barely out of college, young, adventurous, curious and naïve. A more mature woman looking for a threesome would likely go other avenues and not get herself murdered. This case was borderline, but she wanted her revenge badly.

Joanna had rejected her, only to hook up with the next bitch who said yes a few days later.

No one treated Grace that way.

No one.

Edward would have to learn it too.

"It's too dangerous. Come on, lighten up," he said, kissing her hard. "You pick the next one. The next two if you must."

"I already did," Grace said icily. "It only depends on how much of a coward you are."

An instant later, she was holding her stinging cheek.

"Fuck you!"

"There's no time. I want to be out of state by midnight."

"Just this one, please!" Usually, she wouldn't plead with him, or any man, especially after he'd just slapped her, but these were unusual circumstances.

She needed this kill.

Finally, Edward paused in what he was doing. There was pity in his gaze. Moments like this, she hated him with the same passion she had fallen for him.

"What?"

"It's too long. We'd need information, her schedule, the usual. You know."

"Yes." A smile turned the corners of her mouth upwards. He had once called it cruel, and maybe he was right about it. She could still surprise him at times, and he had started killing long before her. "I got all of that."

His eyes widened. "When did you do that?"

"When you were pissing your pants, afraid the police were going to get you. Relax. No one will. Just this one, and we'll leave. I promise. It will be a fucking piece of art, just the way you like it." She could already smell the black marker. Black. Crimson.

His smile matched hers.

"Let me hear it."

Chapter Eight

Rue insisted on paying for the hotel this time, but she drove by each of their apartments to get clothes for an overnight stay. Premeditation, Joanna thought, amused. Happy. That was a scary, unusual place to be, but she couldn't help it.

Rue also wanted to stop at a grocery store.

"Wait here," she said to Joanna, "and whoever calls, don't run away."

"What's the plan?"

"You'll see."

Joanna leaned back into her seat, listening to the wistful song on the radio. She realized she was smiling. If it wasn't the end, it was at the very least a time-out from the ongoing nightmare. Dating somebody, for as long as this could possibly last…She had to think about cleaning up her home along with her mind and making the bed sometime. What a prospect.

Rue returned fifteen minutes later with a couple of bags.

"I'm intrigued."

"Good. Just let me take care of everything for now, okay?"

"I remember what you said about taking the lead. You weren't kidding."

"You okay with that?"

"Absolutely."

That had been missing from her life for a long time, letting someone else take care of things, maybe from the moment Joanna had realized her mother wasn't going to come back. She didn't think it was more than a coincidence—or bad luck for Rue, it could still go either way—that she made that connection now. In any case, it wasn't a good time to go back there.

She was an adult now, in what could at some point become a relationship, and Rue had a surprise for her. Joanna couldn't complain about anything.

This hotel was quite a step up from last night's accommodations, which reminded her once again that Rue's career looked a lot different from the way hers had turned out. Once upon a time, she'd been used to being the one not only to hold doors open but to take care of the check at the end of a restaurant visit. She had enjoyed it. No woman she had seen ever questioned it.

Joanna was questioning herself now, not sure she was comfortable with this new reality, or if this was the reason she had preferred one-night-stands and cheap hotels in the recent past.

"Don't worry," Rue said. "I can afford it. If I couldn't, I'd make you deal with my bathroom situation, but I prefer to invite you into my home once it's all functional again."

"That's okay. Maybe you'd like to come to mine sometime next week?"

"I would, totally. Now let's check out this room."

It was a junior suite with a king bed, a sitting area and an electric fireplace. The window was overlooking the park and the river in the distance.

Now Joanna actually felt ashamed for the place she had taken Rue to. It seemed tacky in comparison.

Joining her at the window, Rue wrapped her arms around her waist.

"Did you hear a single word I said two minutes ago? I want to be here. With you. If we're on the same page, that's all that matters to me."

"We are," Joanna said, surprised by the emotion creeping into her voice. She turned to kiss Rue, the need for closeness almost overwhelming all of a sudden.

"Just a moment," Rue whispered. "There's a little something I'd like to prepare. Can you wait here for me?"

"Barely."

"It will be worth it. I promise."

Moments later, she heard the water running in the bathroom, and then a multitude of other sounds, vague, dream-like. This was a dream. Joanna dreaded the moment she would have to return to reality.

"It's ready," Rue called from the bathroom. Sitting in the armchair by the window, watching the snowflakes fall once more, Joanna had almost dozed off. She got up to walk into the bathroom, her jaw dropping at the sight. The bubble bath she had expected, but not the battery-powered candles, and the tray with glasses of champagne, strawberries, whipped cream, and chocolates. Rue sat in the tub, the bathrobe lying on the counter.

"When did you have the time to whip cream?" Joanna asked if that was the most pressing issue.

"I'm afraid it's from a can. I hope you don't mind, that's the best I could do. Will you join me in here?"

"I can't wait."

It occurred to Joanna that this was the second time in less than twenty-four hours that she was stripping for Rue, and she didn't mind a bit. There was something enticingly innocent and genuine about this scene, even with the clearly seductive theme.

There was comfort in trust, she knew. The time spent in prison had seemed less daunting by small degrees after she met

Kira, and a lot worse after she left. Her friendship with Vanessa had done a great deal to help her settle into the new life, keep the bitterness at an acceptable minimum.

Normally, Joanna took her time, put the people in her life to a test. Suspicion came a lot easier to her than letting her guard down with someone she barely knew, but for some reason, Rue made it easy.

She took in Rue's content expression, her smile full of excitement. "You came up with all of this today?"

"I knew I had to think fast, so you wouldn't elude me again." Rue leaned back, her gaze...self-conscious? Worried? "Is this, am I too much? I mean, maybe that's why that person never showed up. I have this thing for wanting to create the perfect environment, because hell, you never know what's going to happen, and with you it was just so good. It didn't want it too end, but I don't want to make you uncomfortable."

"You're not," Joanna assured her. "In fact, this is so much better than what my evening was going to look like. I'm sorry for freaking out. Now that you've done your homework, I guess you can see why."

"Yeah. I'm glad I could convince you."

They both moved at the same time, meeting for a kiss that soon turned deep and hungry. Joanna closed her eyes as she felt Rue's hand trailing down her side and between her legs.

The scents of chocolate and strawberries would be accompanied by interesting sensations in the future. She allowed herself to step outside of reality for a moment, mistakes made, catastrophe scenarios for the future that were almost always on her mind, to just feel. Joanna hoped Rue would make too much of this, expect this to go somewhere, and then, for long perfect moments she didn't care.

"Wow. You are good for me. I haven't had a cigarette since this morning."

Rue laughed. "I'm not sure what to make of that. Shouldn't you be craving one now?"

"Funny, but all I'm craving is you." She pulled her close again, intent on reciprocating, but Rue shook her head. "Let's go to the bedroom."

Joanna accepted the white towel Rue handed out to her and stepped out of the tub, following her into the bedroom. At this point, she would have followed her anywhere. Maybe it meant that she was learning how to trust again.

❧

Grace knew she would have to go back to the car, otherwise someone might notice her, and Edward wouldn't take kindly to that, on edge as he already was.

She couldn't help herself, even though the window was too high up for her to see anything, and she couldn't even be sure which one it was. She couldn't understand herself. One of them was like the other, usually, bodies to enjoy and dispose of once they were done. This one would be no different, or would she?

It wasn't that she had romantic feelings for Joanna, or that she wanted to give up her life with Edward to do what normal people did, date, settle down, stop thinking about the image of a sharp blade breaking skin, blood welling up.

The salt of tears.

The remembered sensations excited her, almost making her forget that behind one of those windows, Joanna was probably having sex with the woman from The Copper Door. They didn't even make the effort to pass it off for anything else, always going to a hotel. Well, Joanna couldn't possibly bring anyone to that dump her apartment was, and Rue...Grace hadn't been inside her place yet, but she'd seen the contractor's van. She had to come up with a plan, and soon, before Edward changed his mind.

At least he had grudgingly accepted her choice.

Her right. Joanna was going to suffer.

Grace smiled to herself, thinking that this would be nothing new for her. She had accepted the martyr role years ago, a perfect fit. She finally got back into the car.

See you soon.

Chapter Nine

J oanna spent the next few days in utter and complete con-
fusion. She had made plans to see Rue again in a couple
of days, went through her work shifts on autopilot, and spent
most of her time at home cleaning up her apartment, save for
the printouts regarding the case. To her surprise, Theo emailed
her the old file under threats should she ever tell anyone about
it.

She felt almost guilty for letting her mind drift to other
things, as if it invalidated the speech she'd made to Christina.
She was going to drop by after her work shift, before picking
up Rue. The weight of the world didn't seem all that heavy any
longer, though it was scary to think that another person had the
power to do that.

What happened once she wasn't in Joanna's life anymore?
Back to shots with Vanessa and the occasional awkward family
dinner with Kira.

Kira had called and left a message, asking her how things
were. Joanna didn't want to tell her how things were, because
she would completely misinterpret them.

Compartmentalizing was a skill Joanna had never been particularly good at. While she browsed the aisle of local wines at
the liquor store, she wondered why the slasher was back after
going as far as California. Had he grown up here? Made ties to

the community? Coincidence? She decided against the latter. He had managed to evade capture for so long, it was unlikely that anything he did wasn't meticulously calculated. Thinking of her former theories, she was surprised that he would take on a partner, a possible liability.

Who was she? And how disturbed was the woman to be in on the killings? How did he meet her?

What kind of wine would Rue like?

Joanna knew she had done a pretty decent job with the apartment. That didn't hide the fact that it was tiny or hadn't been updated in a while. She hoped that Rue wouldn't pay too much attention and enjoy the company instead, like she had on Sunday afternoon.

The memory of Rue, shivering underneath her, had her stop and catch her breath. She was grateful to her in so many ways she couldn't even convey.

Kira called when she was just inside the apartment.

"Sit down first, please. I'm doing a spontaneous Christmas party this weekend, and no, you can't say no."

Joanna gave the bags on her counter a critical look. Some of the contents would have to go into the fridge.

"Who's coming?" she asked, absent-mindedly.

"That's your first question? I'm amazed. You did hear what I said, right?"

"Yeah, I heard you fine. I'm just in a hurry. I'll have a visitor and I have to prepare dinner." She laughed at the meaningful silence. "Don't get any ideas. It's only dinner."

"For someone you had sex with?"

"None of your business, and yes."

"That's great! Bring her to the party."

"Kira, stop this! I don't even know what her plans are."

"Oh, I knew it. This is the best news ever. You must bring her."

Joanna realized that the course of this conversation was making her uncomfortable.

"No, I don't. I told you, it's just dinner. It doesn't mean anything."

At least, if she believed that, the end of it wouldn't hurt so much. Where did that come from? This was ridiculous. It was only the third time they met.

"Yeah, tell yourself that," Kira scoffed. "Will you come anyway? Please."

"I'll think about it."

"Okay. That's a lot more than I hoped for. I'll see you Saturday, and enjoy dinner with your girlfriend."

"Right." If Kira had been in front of her, Joanna might have taken the childish route and stuck out her tongue.

For some reason, she didn't mind the bantering. She felt a lot more relaxed than she had in a long time, even with that ever-present shadow over her head. It wasn't going away anytime soon. She might as well stop feeding it.

Rue arrived right on time. Joanna took her coat and hung it on the rack. To pre-empt any judgment, she gave her an easy out.

"I know it's not great but take a look around if you like. I guess I should be thinking about renovations as well—or moving."

"Don't worry." Rue kissed her softly, with enough underlying heat to spark recent memories. "I came here for you, not to be nosy. Besides, it looks great. I had to do with less space before I bought the condo."

"I'm relieved. I think. I hope you're a little hungry too because I don't cook all that often. Don't be afraid. It tastes fairly good."

"I'm sure."

Rue's eyes widened at the sight of the candle-lit table.

"What? I can be romantic too."

"I never had any doubts."

It couldn't last, Joanna reminded herself. All of it, every moment, was too good to be true.

Nevertheless, she pulled a chair for Rue and served her some wine. "I'll be right back."

After dinner was on the table, they sat and ate in silence for several minutes before Rue laid down her fork.

"I'm sorry, but I was really hungry. Still am, actually. This tastes great."

"Thank you." Joanna didn't want to go too creative when she hadn't cooked for herself, or anyone, in a while, but the baked chicken had turned out pretty tasty. More than the success, and the cozy warmth of the meal, it was Rue's company that helped her relax in a way she'd almost thought was lost. She was in the moment, not obsessing about what could be, or could have been. This was different.

So, much later, when they had retreated to the sofa bed, she dared to ask.

"Would you like to come to a friend's Christmas party with me?"

"I'd love to," Rue said without hesitation.

꧁꧂

Of course, the reprieve could never last too long. It wasn't in her nature to indulge herself.

Would he, would they come back for Christina? The question haunted Joanna as she lay awake, Rue curled up against her side, sleeping peacefully.

Most predators were cocky, narcissistic, and a victim getting away would hurt their ego. They would want to "rectify" what went wrong in their mind and blame the ones they thought were responsible. Of course, in their minds, someone else was always guilty. Decker had taken out his anger for Mila, for daring to survive, on her friends.

The slasher and his girlfriend, where were they? Had they left town after the last murder, or were they still lying in wait?

In the early days, he had preferred college towns, graduate students and young professionals, but there were never enough similarities to create a pattern. It was rather easy to follow someone's activities online if they weren't particularly careful. Participation in memes and conversations would give someone like the slasher a glimpse into their personal lives, and if some shared personal information...

She hated victim blaming, didn't want to fall into that trap, but some people were too open and trusting with that kind of details.

Rue had researched her story online. Everyone left a footprint. Everyone. She wondered if Theo had thought of asking Christina about her online activities, then shook her head. Of course he had.

It was strange to think of herself at that time, younger, a lot more naïve and hopeful, convinced she could help rid the world of evil like that, one at a time. She had thought she knew better now, after that fateful decision, after those years on the other side of the walls and barbed wire.

Maybe she hadn't changed as much as she imagined. Underneath those experiences, she was still the same woman, struggling to make a difference. For what reason? When had she started giving a damn again? She hadn't even bought cigarettes, or vodka.

Joanna cast a look at the woman in her arms, kissing the top of her head. Rue murmured something in her sleep, holding on tighter.

Oh, right. *Damn.*

"Joanna, great you could make it. You must be Rue."

Coby, Kira's husband, greeted them at the door, admired the small but obviously expensive gift basket Rue had brought, and showed them where to put their coats. To Joanna's surprise, the moment wasn't awkward at all. It made her wonder if she'd imagined all those looks and whispers, the children's skeptical gazes.

Usually, people didn't know how to deal with what she had done, least how to explain it to their children. Joanna didn't know any better, and yet here she found herself in a scene straight out of a Christmas movie.

"Joanna, Rue, you're here! What are you drinking? Rue, could I tempt you into trying my grandma's eggnog recipe?"

"Absolutely. I'm intrigued."

Kira gave Joanna a meaningful smile as she poured two glasses.

"Good. I hope you enjoy yourselves. There's plenty of food, my husband is behind the bar over there and...be merry. I love your dress, by the way."

Joanna had appreciated it too, earlier, though certainly not in the same way Kira did. She took a sip of the eggnog, whistling. "Your Grandma sure came up with a conversation starter. Thanks for having us."

"Oh, you know it's my pleasure. Say hi to Tracey and Anne over there. I think you haven't seen each other in a while." Per explanation for Rue, she said, "We all met when..." and broke off a moment later.

"Kira, Rue knows the story," Joanna came to her rescue. "It took only a few clicks. What we didn't know was that this is the reunion of *Orange is the new Black*." Not everyone had been friendly with an ex-cop, but these women appreciated the fact that she had killed an abusive monster more than anything she'd done before.

Kira laughed. "Joanna, I can tell you found someone very special. She puts up with you and your very questionable humor."

"I like her sense of humor." Rue gave her a long look insinuating it wasn't the only thing she liked about Joanna, who shook her head and went to greet Tracey and Anne. Kira had been better about keeping in touch, then again, she had been the first one to be released, came back to visit each of them. Joanna didn't want to connect with anyone back then, and even now, she was hesitant about the traps relationships and friendships entailed. Kira and Vanessa had been insistent, and now Rue...

"Joanna! When Kira told us you'd come, we didn't believe it." Anne gave her the once over. "Where have you been hiding? You look great."

Tracey nudged her with her elbow. "You remember what else Kira told us? That she was coming with her girlfriend?"

"Oops, sorry." Anne gave her a wink.

"It's all good. You're still working at The Loft?"

"Oh yes. Turns out I have a real talent for selling over-priced clothes to teens, and the pay is good. Sometimes I cannot believe that is actually legal. You're still moving around palettes in that warehouse?"

Joanna shrugged. "It pays the rent." Somewhere during the conversation, she missed the opportunity to correct Anne and let them know Rue wasn't really her girlfriend—she couldn't call it that, yet, and Joanna wasn't sure she wanted to go there. Maybe this small sin of omission had happened for a reason. It didn't matter now.

"What about you, Tracey?"

"Well...I graduated this summer. Found myself a job, so Maddie and I could move into a new apartment. She's doing well in her new school."

"Wow, Tracey, that's amazing!" Joanna had seen another, darker side of Tracey, when she'd been ready to give up, fearing she'd never see her daughter again, give in to the anger all of them had been wrestling with. She was truly happy for the women she had met under less pleasant circumstances, for the steps they had taken.

"It is. You should come by sometime."

"I sure will."

Tracey took out her phone, and they exchanged numbers.

How she compared in this, Joanna wasn't exactly sure. She certainly had some things going for her. She had a job and a roof over her head. She was...wallowing at times, no doubt, and sometimes she wasn't even sure if that had more to do with Decker, the return of the slasher, or the vague knowledge that whatever she did could never erase the grief of the victim's families—or her own.

Then there was Rue. She watched her laugh at something Kira said. There were many more questions she needed to ask, so much more to find out about her, but she knew the most important answers already. Being with Rue put her at ease in a way she hadn't felt in a long time—or ever.

Perhaps that was the eggnog talking. This was strong stuff. She noticed it was snowing again outside. She hoped Rue would like to stay over. They could come up with ways to stay warm...

"I was ready to break out the champagne because you're actually dating, but I have to say she exceeds all my expectations," Kira had come up beside her while Rue had left for the bathroom, Joanna assumed. "Wow. She's cute and smart. How did that happen?"

"Um, you're kind of insulting me right now."

Kira shook her head. "No way. You were just too stubborn, never allowing yourself to go out there and meet someone nice. I wasn't sure that would ever happen, especially with you getting all up into your old colleagues' business. I stand corrected."

"You don't understand. These murders are related to my old case. I had to tell them at least."

"You think they wouldn't have thought of the link without you?"

"Maybe, maybe not. I had to make sure. Besides, it was one of my current colleagues who found Christina."

"Honey, that still doesn't make it your business. You paid your dues. It's time to *live*."

"Maybe you're right."

At the back of her mind, there were still the words Grace had uttered when Joanna had left her. *"Damn weather. I should have stayed in Cali when I had the chance."*

California.

Why hadn't she thought of this before?

"Excuse me," she said. "I need to make a call."

They had first traced the slasher to California, three murders in the larger Los Angeles area, women who had last been seen in bars. One of them had been seen leaving with a man, but the witness couldn't describe him very well. Signs of torture, multiple stab wounds. Then more cases, scattered over the country and many years, until there was a sudden stop. Of course, Joanna hadn't been able to follow the case closely after her arrest, and she'd lost all her resources.

Theo answered on the second ring. Joanna could finally ask the question that was burning on her mind.

"What if he stopped because of me?"

She could picture Theo shake his head.

"Did it occur to you that you might be overestimating yourself?"

"Come on, you know what I mean! He knew I went to prison. The game wasn't fun any longer. Now that I'm out, he starts killing again, waiting for me to take the bait."

"That's a long shot," Theo said doubtfully. "You've been out for a while. Besides, he can't be sure you're taking that bait."

He could, after the Decker case, after seeing what her life had become. If someone paid attention, they knew she wasn't the same anymore, the cop who made sure that every T was crossed and every I dotted. She was more dangerous, and more of a challenge these days, or at least she could be if she'd been crazy enough to immerse herself any deeper.

He was waiting. And he'd be killing again and again.

"They were in California before they came here. Some of the early victims were in the greater L.A. area. Check with LAPD, okay?"

"I will, thank you. You keep doing whatever it is you're doing, and if you can think of anything else, let me know. This time, we'll get him," he promised.

Joanna wondered if he realized what he'd just said. She, for one, was completely on board with it.

Finally, she found Rue.

"You should really try something from the buffet," she suggested. "Everything is amazing."

"I'm sure, but there's something I need to do first. I'm really sorry I left you alone for so long."

"That's okay. Your friends are nice. I've had some good conversations."

"Well, yeah, I think I can do better."

Rue let herself be pulled onto the makeshift dance floor, and just like that, Joanna felt like she was back in the present moment, whatever ghosts haunting her staying on the periphery.

"Yeah, this is better," Rue whispered. "You know, I'm so grateful to the woman who never showed up. I should send her flowers as a thank you."

"Let's not go that far." Over Rue's shoulder, she caught Kira's gaze. Her friend was giving her the thumbs-up.

Despite their plans which they hadn't talked about in so many words, but silently agreed on, they were one of the last couples to leave the house. Joanna went to get both their coats, noticing something slip out of Rue's.

"I think that belongs to us."

"Oh, lucky you saw that." Kira's husband bent down to pick up the business card and gave it to Joanna. "There you go. Come back soon."

"We will. Happy Holidays."

She could have just put the card back, but curiosity got the better of her. It took a few seconds before realization set in, and the pieces came together. Joanna hastily put the card back into Rue's coat pocket, telling herself that she couldn't have a loud confrontation in her friend's home.

Why even make such a drama out of it? She had known it couldn't last—Joanna just hadn't expected the reason.

Rue had told her that she was working for someone whose political views clashed with hers, but she had kept it vague. An older businessman. She had neglected to mention that said businessman was Lawrence Mitchell, Joanna's father.

Rue had done her homework on Joanna. There was no way she didn't know.

Chapter Ten

"Please, let me explain." Silence ensued as they were walking on the sidewalk, in the general direction of Joanna's apartment, convincing Joanna with each passing second that there was really nothing Rue could explain. "I saw him mentioned in one of the articles I read about you, but I didn't really think it mattered. Then I was afraid you wouldn't want to see me anymore if you knew...I swear I've been looking for another job, but it's not that easy. And he isn't one of the worst."

"Let me be the judge of that. Do you know how many times he came to visit me in prison? Not once."

"That's terrible, but it has nothing to do with us!"

"Is that so? You're not going to take me to office parties or introduce me to your colleagues."

"We weren't there yet," Rue defended herself. "Besides, I didn't think these things mattered to you so much."

"I haven't been in the closet in over twenty years, and I have no intention of going back there. He doesn't know, right? Because there's no way in hell he would have hired you."

"Joanna, that's work. Okay, he doesn't know, but who cares? I've been to hotels and bars with you. I don't care!"

"Well, that's too bad, because I do. You should have told me the moment you knew."

Rue kept her gaze straight ahead, but Joanna had seen the tears glistening in her eyes.

"I don't understand. I work for him. You of all people should understand that we make compromises. He should have been there for you."

"You're right, it doesn't matter. The thing is I'm so fed up with being lied to. I don't want that in my life anymore, and for sure, I don't want him in my life anymore. I'm sorry."

"Joanna, don't do this."

"You haven't given me a good reason why not."

"What do you want?" There was surprising anger in Rue's words. "Give up a career I've been working hard for in the past few years? I know you did that, but Joanna, you have to realize not everyone can go that far for a principle. Do I like the philosophy of this company? Hell, no. I just don't see how it would help anyone if I lost my paycheck and my condo tomorrow. I didn't tell you the truth because I could guess it was complicated between you two. In the years I've worked there, he never mentioned you. I'm so sorry," Rue added quickly when she seemed to realize that those words had hit home with Joanna.

"You know what, I'll take a cab from here. I'll call you tomorrow, and I hope we can talk?"

"Yeah, sure," Joanna said, because it was the fastest way to end this conversation.

❦

She could remove herself from the situation, try to ignore what it meant, but Joanna couldn't get away from the memories, the experiences that had shaped her.

Back then, Mila had gotten away. Joanna and Theo vowed she'd be his last victim. Together with Mila, they were working hard to locate Decker, and the young woman's determination to return to life was helpful. She brought them more details bit by bit, and so they traced his steps while making sure Mila was safe.

Eventually, she went back to college, moved past the notoriety, and made new friends she invited to her home.

Decker found them before Joanna and Theo found him.

Joanna would never forget walking into the place, the notion that something horrible had happened here hitting her with the first step across the threshold. She almost gagged, even though the smell of the blood came a moment later. In the dining area, the table was set, homemade pizza, beer, wine. Four bodies. In another room, a paramedic was tending to Mila who was near catatonic, shaking so hard her teeth clicked together. Joanna didn't think she recognized them at all, her eyes fixed on something only she could see, something even more horrible.

"Are you okay?" Theo asked. He looked like he was going to be sick.

"No." Joanna shook her head. It would be a long time before she'd be close to okay again, if ever. She took a breath, not too deep. "Okay. Let's do this."

They went back into the killing room, talked to the techs still at work, looking for clues. Decker was careful. He had no known associates and hadn't contacted his wife since Mila escaped, and his identity became known to the press.

Joanna could only imagine what the headlines would be.

"This shouldn't have happened. Why didn't we know he was going there? He's like a Goddamn ghost, no traces anywhere."

"I think he might have gone into the mountains," one of the uniforms said. He had been outside, knocking on doors, his cheeks reddened from the cold.

"In this weather?" Joanna asked doubtfully.

"He can't risk a standoff now. He knows he's not going to make it out alive," Theo surmised.

"Still. He has a gun, and he needs to hide somewhere. I want to make sure it's not with anyone around here. Let's check that everyone's doors are locked."

Something Theo had said, stuck in her mind. He's not going to make it out alive. That wasn't the worst scenario, in Joanna's opinion. In fact, she didn't think he deserved to live—but she was also aware that this was an emotional, knee-jerk reaction. She'd put it aside and do her job, as always.

It might have worked out that way if it wasn't for that anonymous tip, someone who had seen Decker going into a cabin close to his. Decker's wife later claimed that she didn't know about it, and they could never prove otherwise.

Once Joanna knew, the decision was surprisingly quick and easy. Mila was talking, but her recovery would take much longer, and the goals had changed drastically from before. She was still in psychiatric care. Not all the funerals for Decker's victims had been held when Joanna set out to stake out the place. It didn't take long for Decker to show up. He was that cocky, thought himself safe.

He thought he was safe even when he opened the door to her, unarmed, laughing as he recognized her.

And then it was over.

Only it wasn't. It might be that Vanessa's beliefs in a functioning system were so strong, or that she was very ambitious—truth be told, Joanna had done a shitty job covering up her tracks. She couldn't seem to find the energy to put into it, and so the day came when Internal Affairs Inspector Young knocked on her door and arrested her.

It wasn't over even then, and Joanna learned that nothing she had done could erase the images, for her, or Mila. It didn't work that way.

Theo didn't visit her, which was a disappointment. Not seeing her father once during the entire time was something Joanna had expected, which didn't mean it didn't hurt. Vanessa came regularly, exorcising demons of her own.

There was too much time, too much darkness, too much opportunity to think.

It wasn't like Joanna had caused a big scandal at the college by having a girlfriend. It was her bad luck that the president played golf with her father.

The payments stopped. She was lucky enough to be able to cover her expenses with a second job and student loans. Then the holidays came around, and she received a short email that said she didn't need to bother coming home that year—or ever—until she had her "sickness" sorted out. Joanna went back only once to get clothes and other items that belonged to her.

Lawrence Mitchell was at a meeting, the housekeeper told her. She sent a letter once, trying to explain, and never got an answer. It turned out to be the most humiliating experience of her life, and remembering it, perhaps it was just as well that he never showed up in prison. Her life could hardly get worse, but the potential was always there.

Tracey felt exhausted, but happy as she rummaged in her purse for her keys, about to unlock her front door after a long day at work. She mused about the chance of meeting Joanna at Kira's, a new woman by her side. She felt proud of what all of them had accomplished, against tougher odds than many other people faced. They had all managed to pull themselves together, start a new life that wouldn't be determined by the people that had hurt them.

They had won, and day by day, she was building a future not only for herself, but for Maddie. It was kind of late, but Tracey hoped she'd still be awake so she could read her bedtime story after sending the babysitter home.

Lost in thought, she never noticed the man coming up behind her until she sensed a presence, and a moment later, the pressure of cold steel against her back.

"Don't scream, or I swear I'll pull the trigger."

In a heartbeat, everything you owned could be taken away. She followed every command mechanically, her only relief that he was dragging her away from the door. Maddie and Jill, the babysitter, would be safe. That was all that mattered.

⁂

Joanna was aware she might have overreacted. Learning that Rue worked for Lawrence had knocked the wind out of her, and she couldn't bring herself to get over that first impulse and do something, call Rue, apologize.

She had been somewhat honest at least, admitting she was working for someone whose convictions were contrary to her own, and that it weighed on her. The rest was unfortunate. She couldn't have known how bad Joanna's history with her father, or both her parents, was.

Maybe it was the occasion Joanna had been waiting for, the way out before someone got hurt. The problem was, she wasn't feeling any better, on the contrary.

At three in the morning, three nights in a row, she was sitting up over those printouts, crying, drinking, feeling like a complete failure—again. This wasn't doing anything for Mila, or Christina. Why couldn't she make that connection?

Why couldn't she let herself be happy?

Rue called several times, but after the third day, the calls stopped. "You know where to find me," she said in the last message. "I feel like a stalker. If you'd like to talk to me, please call."

Joanna didn't call her back, ignoring all hope and intuition. She hadn't managed to maintain a long-term relationship in years. It was ridiculous to think that under the current circumstances, she could do better.

There was no one she could bother with her problems. Her friends had families, lives. Unlike her, they had put the past behind them.

She woke up like many other mornings, alone, hung over, feeling sorry for herself. Joanna spent considerable time in a long hot shower, missing a call from Kira who'd left a message, saying it was urgent.

When Joanna called her back, Kira picked up on the first ring. At first, Joanna had trouble making sense of her words.

"Something terrible happened!"

Kira didn't freak out over nothing. Joanna had an instant bad feeling about this, even before Kira said tearfully, "Tracey is missing. The police called me because they found my name in her day planner, and..."

"What? Kira, calm down. Tell me everything you know."

Joanna realized the phone in her hand was shaking. This couldn't happen. Tracey, like herself, wasn't the slasher's type. He always went for younger women, then again...Tracey had gone back to school and graduated recently. What if he and Grace were changing their MO?

"She didn't come home from work. People saw her leave there, and...that's all I know. Joanna, what are we gonna do?"

The question chilled Joanna to her bones. It implied that Kira was thinking of, fearing the same thing.

"I'll go over there before work, see if I can find out something. I'll call you if I find anything, okay?"

"Okay. Thank you."

Joanna found out half an hour later that she wasn't familiar with the cops at Tracey's house, and they had no intention of letting her in. She called Theo and got his partner Allison Kato instead.

"Can I talk to him? It's urgent."

"Joanna." Theo sounded resigned, and that was enough to set off alarm bells.

"You found her? Is she okay?"

"What are you talking about?" Now, resignation was creeping into his tone.

"Tracey Miller. She's missing, and she's a friend of mine. What makes you think it's not related?"

"What makes you think it is? There's an investigation, but as far as I know, Miller didn't hook up with couples after work. There's no reason to assume—"

"Please. You can't rule it out, okay? You know that this has become personal a while ago. I'm on their radar."

"I'm afraid that's true, so I'd appreciate it if you let me do my job. I'm sorry about your friend, but everyone is doing the best they can. Later, Joanna."

Another night, another nightmare, only the stakes had risen. She had never felt so useless.

How could he and Grace know, unless they had been following her every step right from the start?

Joanna printed out a map and marked the places where Christina and Tracey lived, where Christina had been held, where Felicity was murdered. It was all random. They worked with opportunity, an abandoned house, a noisy motel. Still no word on their means of transportation.

She didn't know what to do, other than drown once more in the memories.

❦

108

In the morning, Kato called her. It wasn't much of a surprise to Joanna when she said,

"An officer let me know you were at Tracey Miller's apartment, asking about her."

"Don't tell me I should step away. This is my friend we're talking about." Joanna had a guilty moment acknowledging that she wouldn't have met Tracey again if it wasn't for Kira's party. Probably, she wouldn't have made the effort.

It didn't matter now.

Detective Kato sighed. "Slow down for a moment, okay? It's not him who took her."

"How do you know that?"

"Because we found her."

"What? Where? I need to—"

"Joanna, breathe. She'll be okay, but she doesn't want to see anyone at the moment, and I hope you respect that. It was her ex. He waited for her at the front door, pulled a gun on her and made her come with him."

"Oh God."

"He slapped her and yelled at her for leaving him." Allison's tone revealed her disgust clearly. She sounded more resigned when she continued. "She feels ashamed. Ironic, isn't it?"

"I'd call it sad. What about Maddie? Is she okay?"

"The babysitter stayed with her until Tracey's mom could take her. It won't be long before Tracey can go home. As for the guy, we put him away. We found drugs and unregistered weapons in the apartment, so he won't bother her in the near future."

Joanna bit her lip. She knew Tracey didn't have the best of relationships with her mother, but at least she had shown up.

"All right. Thank you."

"No problem. She needs some space right now. She'll call you when she's ready."

"Okay."

Joanna remained standing in the same spot for a moment, then gave in to a lesser impulse and punched the wall, her knuckles stinging instantly. *He won't bother her in the near future*. What about a few years down the line? *She feels ashamed*. Why was it that women kept carrying that burden when they had done nothing to bring this kind of situation upon them?

Joanna felt ashamed, too, for her life slipping out of her control bit by bit. She did her work shifts mechanically, coming home to drink and obsess, on the case, the world in general, the chance she might have had with Rue, and blown. Too little too late to blame any of it on her absent parents.

She fell asleep on the couch before midnight, woken again by the phone.

"Leave me alone," she mumbled to no one, but picked up anyway, too late. The answering machine had already picked up.

"Hey, I'm Jeff."

"Good for you. Wrong number." She was about to delete the message, when the next words made her reconsider.

"I'm the bartender at The Copper Door. You asked to tell me if that certain lady came around. Well, she did."

For long moments, she just sat and listened to the message, twice, three times. She should have done something, get up and go talk to him, call Theo and inform him about a possible lead, but Joanna lacked the energy to do any of it. The confrontation with the past, again and again in recent days, had drained her. She wanted to keep hiding, from the world, her failures, but of course that wasn't an option. It never had been.

She pushed herself off from the couch and put on her coat to walk to The Copper Door. It was probably closed for cleaning at this time, but Jeff had said she could find him there until three a.m. It was four minutes to three when she arrived, shivering because as usual, she hadn't bothered with a scarf or gloves. The place was dark, just a couple of cars in the lot, the street empty at this time of night. Joanna wondered briefly if this was a trap, and "Jeff" was actually in on the plan. It wasn't like she'd ever learned the bartender's name in the first place. Somebody might have overheard her talking to him or...

"Hey. Joanna it is, right?"

Apparently, he was more observant than she had been.

"Jeff. You said you had news about the girl?"

"Yeah, she stopped by earlier. Changed her hair too, she's a redhead now. She mentioned that she'd like to see you again."

"What did you tell her?" Joanna asked, alarmed.

"Nothing. She brought it up, said you'd forgotten to exchange phone numbers." His tone was devoid of judgment. He had probably seen it all.

"Do you know where I can find her?"

"She said she's staying with a friend, but if you come around every once in a while, she'd try to catch up with you."

"Think. This is important. Did she mention the friend's name, or any hint as to where she is now?"

"Wow, you're eager to find her. I'm sorry, no. You said to call in case she showed up."

"Yeah, thank you for that." Joanna pulled her coat tighter around her. "When exactly was she here? Did you see if she had a car? Went with someone?"

"Hey, slow down. I *work* here, remember? I listen to the stories people tell me, but where they're going afterwards is none of my business. She was here around midnight. I called you when I had a moment. I can't tell you anything else. If you'll excuse me now?"

"Yeah. Sure. Thanks again."

He unlocked one of the cars with his key, climbed inside and drove away. Joanna stood in the same place, cursing herself and the world in general. Three hours. Grace could be anywhere by now. She had no doubt that everything she'd told Jeff was some sort of message. If she wanted to see Joanna again, it certainly wasn't for socializing. She was playing a game. It was dangerous for her and her partner to stay in town, yet she couldn't seem to stay away. If part of that temptation had to do with Joanna, so be it.

The longer they hung around, the more likely it was for the police to catch them. After all, Theo didn't inform Joanna about every new development. She had to let him know, in any case—and then go back to her cold, lonely world. Or maybe not in that order.

She could have called Rue…That probably wasn't a good idea, considering the time of night, and Grace's message. Once this mess was cleared up, maybe there would be a chance to talk to her again. Joanna wasn't so sure.

Back home, she left a message for Theo, then went back to the printouts still spread out all over the place. California. Grace. Jeff. The slasher. She wished she'd still had the resources that were available to her in her old job. As it was, she had become a wannabe, an amateur trying to make do. That went for her professional life in particular, but also for the rest of it. She couldn't seem to win.

Joanna finished the bottle of vodka with resentful thoughts of her father and Decker who had made such a mess of what had once seemed a promising path, and finally fell asleep past five a.m., when the phone rang.

"Hey, friend," Theo said, his tone unusually cheery. "Thank you. I want you to know I love you."

"What the—" Her head hurt. "Are you drunk?"

That should have been his question.

"I'm elated. Get up and get your ass over here. I have something to show you."

"Tone it down, please. What's going on?"

"We've done pretty good work if I may say so, but your tips were the icing on the cake. It's almost over. We found Grace Lester."

"What?" Joanna sat up abruptly, holding her head the next moment. "What about the guy?"

"Not yet, but she'll soon realize that giving him up is her only chance. I want you here. You might be able to help us."

"Me? How?"

"She likes you. I know you can be very convincing, and with your history..." For the first time, his tone was a bit more sober, almost apologetic. "It's worth a shot. She might go for it."

"What are you saying, that she and I have something in common?"

"It's not what I was saying, but she might see it that way. I want you here in no more than fifteen minutes."

"Sheesh, relax, I'm not getting paid for this anymore."

"Yet, you can't stay away."

"I guess that's true. I'll see you in a few."

Joanna disconnected the call, almost managing a smile, but only until she went to the bathroom and saw her face in the mirror. The past days of binging and feeling sorry for herself showed in the most unattractive ways. She took a deep breath. Maybe Grace would be a little more open if she thought Joanna had missed her badly. Funny how she had gone from the department's biggest disappointment, *persona non grata*, to someone whose help they could use. Joanna was careful to think her luck could have changed. Every time, she'd ended up in a space worse than before. It was better not to hope altogether.

Chapter Eleven

R ue felt like living on the edge. All her life, playing it safe, avoiding conflicts at all costs, had it really served her?

Joanna was ignoring her calls. Rue still had no idea what exactly had gone wrong. She had kept one little detail from Joanna, true. She'd thought it didn't matter all that much when Mitchell never talked about his daughter—or his family, for that matter.

She had learned via the company gossip that he was dating a younger woman, a conservative political consultant she'd seen at the office a few times. Rue had a hard time understanding why he felt so entitled to mess with other people's families when his own was hardly a model, but in the years she'd worked for him, she had learned to smile and keep her thoughts to herself.

She wasn't sure she could do this any longer. The need for change and atonement had haunted her even before she'd met Joanna in the dingy bar, but it was now stronger than ever. Rue had a couple of job interviews lined up. There was a chance for her to leave quietly, without stirring up things that were better left untouched.

She wanted answers though, to understand what happened between her and Joanna. Rue had contemplated the conversation a few times in her head, sure she'd never go all the way, because that would be...crazy.

"Can I ask you a personal question?" It was long after hours, and she and Mitchell were the only ones left at the office. She had made coffee for both of them, a task that still fell on her and always would.

Lawrence Mitchell looked up from his impressive teak desk. There were no personal photos on it, just folders, balances and the occasional file of an employee. While making record profits, the company had a high employee turnover.

"Since I'm obviously ruining your holidays, I think one personal question is fair," he said, smiling good-naturedly. "Sit."

"Thank you, sir." She was likely to commit career suicide. Even with the upcoming interviews, she'd take a pay cut. Rue had been waiting so long, she was afraid that if she didn't take that step soon, she'd work for Mitchell's until retirement. Even so, it was a gamble. "I met your daughter recently."

Mitchell gave no indication how this affected him, if at all. "Is that so?"

"Yes. I was just wondering..."

"Curious," he substituted.

"That too. I imagine it must have been difficult for you."

For the first time since she had brought up the subject, Mitchell showed a flicker of emotion.

"Difficult? My dear Rue, you have no idea. How do you think a father reacts in that situation? She probably told you a very different version of the story, but no matter what she is saying these days, I always tried to help her. She rejected all of it, refused to come to her senses. I did the only thing I could do."

"I saw some of the articles. I can't even begin to think..."

To her surprise, he laughed, shaking his head. Rue detected a hint of bitterness.

"What? No, I didn't care what they wrote. Decker was one deranged individual. I'm fine with the fact that she blew that bastard away. Problem is, before and after prison, she refused to give up her immoral lifestyle. I only had her best interests in mind, but she never wanted to listen, and look at her now, hauling around crates at a warehouse, no husband, no children."

Rue tried not to cringe too hard—after all, she had no husband or children to present either, and she found Mitchell's attitude disgusting...but she still had to hold out for a few days.

"Well, not every woman wants children. Maybe she actually is happy."

If Joanna wasn't, it had little to do with her sexual orientation.

"Happy? She might delude herself into thinking that, but it's sick. She'll wake up one day and realize that, but then it'll be too late."

"So, you think I'm sick too?"

For a few seconds, there was a silent standoff. Rue held her breath, thinking it was no secret any longer how exactly she'd met Joanna. In a heartbeat, she had confirmed all of Mitchell's stereotypes—and he could actually fire her for it, if he wanted to. Who was she kidding? He had cut off his own daughter.

"I'll pretend I didn't hear that. Frankly, I don't want to know about you, or Joanna. Why don't you call it a night and come back tomorrow with a fresh perspective, and never ask me about her again?"

There was a clear warning to his words. Rue ignored all the red flags.

"You never went to see her in prison because she's a lesbian? That's cold. Why would you do that to her...to yourself, choose ideology over your own blood?"

"That's enough!" Lawrence Mitchell raised his voice just enough to make her flinch. "This is none of your darn business, lady. Stay out of it, I'm warning you. You could be out on the street today, and I could make it very difficult for you to even get a job interview in this town. I think it's best you go home and calm down."

Rue got to her feet.

"Well, thanks for the conversation. I think you're the one who's going to have regrets sometime soon, but you're right, it's none of my business. What's my business is if my work supports dangerous prejudice like yours. I'm not going to do that any longer. I quit."

He shook his head, smiling, his composure radiating condescendence.

"Good night, Rue. I expect you here tomorrow at eight. You know, I'm old enough to remember a time when women knew their place, and when to speak. I long for those days."

Rue walked out, knowing she could never return and still look at herself in the mirror. She was thrilled and terrified at the same time.

She wished Joanna would answer her phone.

❧

"Rough night?" Theo asked after taking a first look at her.

Joanna shrugged, thinking that there was no reason to tell him that it had only been one of a few rough nights.

"Merry Christmas," she said instead. "Any closer to finding the guy?"

"Not yet. All right, let's talk about this. You know the drill. You'll be safe, I'll be in the room with you, and she'll be cuffed. Don't get too close anyway. Don't provoke her, just try to convince her of what's the best option."

Joanna listened to his speech with a blank stare. "What part of this do you think is new to me? I used to work here, remember?"

"Oh, I do remember. Let's get this done, okay?"

Joanna followed him to the interrogation room, the relief she'd felt after hearing Grace was arrested, vanishing quickly. What had happened to her? She had made questionable choices before, but hooking up with a serial murderer was on a whole new level. She'd been let down by her instincts, or maybe she had come to ignore them in favor of evasion and denial.

Grace looked up at her, obviously excited to see her.

"Joanna! I'm surprised they let you in, with your history and all, but I'm glad you're here. I hope you told them it's all some misunderstanding."

Joanna studied her, feeling nothing but disgust for the woman, and herself.

"Come on, we both know it's everything but. You're smart. If you don't want to listen to them, listen to me. I'm not a cop anymore, but I'm telling you this: You have to give him up. It's the only way."

Grace's laugh was fake all the way. "Give up who, honey? You're still mad at me I suggested a threesome to you? You would have enjoyed it, I promise you."

"I don't know. Too many girls you suggested a threesome to turned up dead."

"That's a sad coincidence. Do you think those killers are the only people with an exciting sex life?"

"You call killing exciting?"

For a split-second, there was a gleam in Grace's eyes that told Joanna everything she needed to know. Not a confession...but a start.

"Don't put words in my mouth. What I mean is, other people have threesomes, and hook-ups. Just because I made that offer to you, you can't think I'm a murderer, or my boyfriend is."

"Where is he now, your boyfriend? You think he's going to bail you out—or maybe skip town?"

"Why would he? We have nothing to hide."

"You were seen leaving a club with a young woman named Felicity who was found dead."

"Well...apparently, she got some more action that night, I don't know. We didn't kill her."

Joanna sighed. "You know, I don't have to be here. I came to do you a favor, because I was pretty sure you wouldn't believe the cops. You play it the way you want to, but they're closing in on him anyway, and once they find him...Let's say you must trust this guy a lot to think that he wouldn't let you take the fall."

"You're wasting your time," Grace spat. "They have nothing. So, we hooked up with the girl that night, that's not proving anything. They will have to let me go soon either way."

"Yeah, maybe." Joanna leaned back in her chair. "What about DNA? Were you always that careful?"

"What DNA? Are you stupid? We had sex with her, of course there's DNA...What are you talking about?"

Joanna could tell Grace was rattled. She figured that was all she could do for now.

"He couldn't resist coming back to that motel, could he? For old times' sake? It's important to clean up the scene. I didn't do that. I guess you guys are better planners, otherwise...The police might still find something. That's none of my concern though, is it? My job is done here. Bye, Grace. Nice seeing you again."

She hoped Grace would call her back, but the woman remained in her sullen silence. Joanna hoped Theo's enthusiastic wake up call meant they had all their ducks in a row to keep Grace in custody regardless of her claims.

The alternative was chilling.

Joanna was certain that the woman she'd slept with not long ago was an accomplice to the murders. There was no sign she'd been coerced into any of it.

Killing, to her, was exciting. She had given herself away in that moment.

❦

"You planted some doubts, good. You saw how she lit up when you said killing is exciting?"

"Yeah, unfortunately that's not enough. Please, tell me that you have enough. She's not going anywhere, right?"

"If the DNA testing comes back on time, and it should, we'll be fine."

"You still don't have the results?"

"You remember. It's not like on TV when they snap their fingers, and bam! Results."

"Yeah. I suppose you don't need me anymore."

"You did good, Joanna. Thank you."

"You're welcome."

Walking back to her car, Joanna realized that for a few minutes, she had forgotten that this wasn't part of her day job, that she'd been invited for a brief time only to get a reality check on her way out. She didn't belong here. In fact, she had a work shift coming up in two hours, regardless of the fact that it was Christmas Eve. Today would most likely decide the fate of both Grace and her boyfriend, the slasher, but she wouldn't be around for any of it.

Joanna allowed herself the fantasy of a different life, where she'd never made it her personal mission to avenge the deaths of Decker's victims, and still somehow, miraculously still met Rue. She wasn't quite sure what role her parents would play in this scenario, if any.

She closed the blinds in her bedroom and tried to let sleep drown out the harrowing doubts.

Nightmares woke her up hours later, most of them vague, though she remembered running, a small strip of land under her feet, the flood catching up with her. In some way, feeling competent and needed for a few hours was cruel, dangling a life in front of her she couldn't have anymore.

Because of the choices she'd made.

Joanna cast a look at the clock on the nightstand. She was supposed to be at work now. There was a better place to lick her wounds and drown her sorrows. She called in sick and headed straight for The Copper Door.

Vanessa was already sitting at the counter when she came in, a Martini in front of her.

"Hey. What are you doing here?" Joanna asked, sitting on the stool beside her.

"What do you think? Theo won't be coming home anytime soon. Everyone's on the lookout for Lester's boyfriend, and I didn't want to sit around in my apartment feeling useless."

"That makes two of us. I'm sorry. Not the way you wanted to spend Christmas."

"What about you? I thought you were seeing that cute—"

"It didn't work out," Joanna said brusquely, already knowing Vanessa wouldn't be satisfied with her answer.

"What do you mean it didn't work out? How can you know after such a short time? Did you even try?" She scoffed. "Who am I kidding? There I thought you'd changed."

"It's not that easy," Joanna defended herself. "I found out she works for my father."

"So what? Somebody's bound to work for him. Homophobes have lives too."

"If you work for them, that means you support them. You don't have to openly support them."

"And maybe you just have to pay the rent. Seriously, that's all?"

"She knew who I was...and who he was, and she didn't tell me. You...you know. He never once came, and you know why? It never mattered to him that I killed a man, that was all good and righteous. He couldn't get over the fact that I'm a lesbian."

"I understand he hurt you. Rue didn't. She probably had no idea about his toxic behavior. Why don't you give her a chance?"

"Because I don't want her to get hurt!" Joanna was shocked to realize how close she was to tears. Maybe this was for the best. The past days, Rue, the confrontation with her father's prejudice, had weakened her, crushed her resolve. This wasn't healthy. She wanted to go back to the woman who knew what she was doing and took the risk even if it didn't turn out well for her. Because it had been righteous. "Forget about it." She signaled Jeff who came over to take her order, a beer and a shot of vodka.

"Celebrating something?" Vanessa asked sarcastically.

"It's Christmas. Theo made an arrest. I'm free again. Take a pick."

"Yeah, about that." Vanessa took a sip of her Martini. "Lester's got a lawyer. She'll probably make bail."

"Fuck," Joanna said, because nothing else came to mind.

"Yeah, my sentiments exactly. Maybe they're lucky, and the DNA results are going to nail her. I don't get it. If my boyfriend got into some bad shit, I wouldn't enable him in the first place, but if I was her, I'd save myself first. Does that make me the bigger psychopath?"

"You're not a psychopath. You have very clear standards when it comes to wrong and right."

Vanessa regarded her for a long time before she spoke. It occurred to Joanna that the Martini probably wasn't the first. She downed her shot and waved her fingers at Jeff for another one which he promptly provided.

"If you could go back, do you think you would have made different choices?" Vanessa asked.

The image of the bodies in Mila's apartment flashed on Joanna's mind.

"What about you?"

"I asked you first."

"I don't know. I don't think so. I was...driven. From the moment I had made that decision, I knew I couldn't go back. I thought that would make it all stop, the nightmares, the doubts, everything."

"And, did it?"

"No. Not for me, or Mila...but I know for sure he isn't out there anymore, preying on other women. That's one less. All right, your turn."

Jeff dutifully sat another shot glass in front of her, and another Martini for Vanessa who contemplated her answer.

"Maybe. I still believe I did the right thing—I know I did, by the law anyway, and I think the law matters, otherwise we could all do whatever we wanted. I just don't think putting you in prison served anyone."

"I made some friends," Joanna offered, prompting Vanessa to laugh.

"Yeah. Way to go."

"If you want to know whether it did the trick, I guess you're right. Nothing changed. I don't feel much remorseful. I wish we'd live in a world where we'd never have to make decisions like that. Where there aren't any assholes that kill and torture women for recreation."

Vanessa made a face as if sick, taking another sip of her drink. And another. Joanna wasn't the only one who had a lot on her mind.

"If it makes you feel any better," she continued, "I'm not traumatized. Not by that, anyway. I didn't go to prison for something I didn't do. By the letter of the law, you were right...so there's that."

"I still have doubts sometimes," Vanessa confessed. "But I know, at the end of the day, I was doing my job. I had to, if the integrity of our profession means anything, that the people can trust that there are places we'll never go. I think you should call Rue. Coming home to someone...it helps. With the doubts and the nightmares."

"Yeah, I don't think that's going to happen anytime soon. Let's face it. I'm just not good relationship material."

"I think you have a bit of a martyr complex sometimes."

Joanna wondered whether she should be offended and decided to laugh instead. Vanessa joined in.

"We are pathetic," she said with emphasis.

"Yeah, speak for yourself."

"I thought you really liked her."

"I did. It happens."

"You don't think you could forgive her?"

"I already have," Joanna said. "That's not the point."

Vanessa groaned and drank the last sip of her Martini.

"For years, I've been coming here to drink with you, and sometimes I think I still don't get you at all."

Joanna didn't know how to answer that. To be honest, she didn't know herself all that well. She hadn't known what she was capable of until the moment arrived. She had seen things that had changed her, in her job and then while serving her time. If it wasn't for Kira, she might have given up somewhere along the line, simply go under.

"Stop trying," she advised. "There's not much to know."

"Call her," Vanessa insisted. "How do you figure things could get any worse? At least you'd try and stick it to your old man. If you give up, you're letting him win."

It was a theory, but cutting Joanna out of his life wasn't a game for Lawrence. He was dead serious and self-righteous about it.

At times, she felt like she was living a self-fulfilling prophecy—her life wasn't exactly holding up to anyone's high moral standards, although that had nothing to do with her sexual orientation. But if she had been straight, and approached relationships the way she did, he still might have shunned her, because he was old-fashioned that way. If she'd been the son he always wanted, every indiscretion would be easily forgiven, but she had disappointed him from day one.

"I'll try. Tomorrow. I swear."

That might make her a liar, come tomorrow, but she wanted Vanessa off her back and Rue out of her mind for a moment. She had wasted enough time of her life wondering what could have been.

No more.

"Don't give me that look," she said to Jeff when catching his hesitation. "I'll be walking home."

"You don't want to share a cab?" Vanessa chimed in.

"No thanks. You're on the other side of town. It's just a few blocks. I'll be fine."

"Are you sure?"

"Yes, I am. Now could you both cut it out? Just one more and I'll go home."

"Yeah, me too," Vanessa agreed. "Call me tomorrow. Right after you call her. I want to know."

Joanna was aware of Jeff regarding them curiously before he turned to another customer. He might be wondering about things that were none of his business...She couldn't care less. As long as he kept his fantasies to himself—if everyone did that, the world would be a much better place.

"I'll see you," she said, meaning both Vanessa and Jeff, then she bundled herself up in her coat to face the cold outside. She could see Vanessa taking out her phone and calling a cab, then she focused on the sidewalk in front of her. Rain and rapidly dropping temperatures had led to black ice in places, and she had to be careful not to slip. Being drunk and wrestling with a dark past and an uncertain future didn't make things easier. Joanna stopped at the red light, behind her a mixed group of night owls waiting for the nightline, the last bus that went by these streets.

Would this damn red light never change? She was freezing and feeling uncomfortably crowded at the same time. Regardless of the time, she might have a hot bath once home, preferably with a night cap. The night before the moment of truth...

How the hell could Grace get a lawyer? Would they do a background check on him too? They didn't yet know enough about her either. If she had money to throw around, that might make everything even more complicated.

Maybe she'd stop thinking about these things so much if she had someone to come home to. Even if things hadn't become messy between her and Rue, it had been much too early for that kind of notion. Too early, too late...it seemed like Joanna had lost any sense of timing.

She was jolted out of her thoughts roughly when a hand pushed her hard and onto the street. Joanna heard cries, a horn and screeching brakes close enough to hurt her ears, and then someone pulled her back seconds before the night bus came to a halt. The driver opened his door and came rushing out.

"Jesus! What the hell...are you okay?"

For long seconds, she couldn't breathe, the scenery around her graying out before it stabilized again. Joanna realized that there was blood on her hands, and a tear to her jeans.

"I'm okay." The words finally came, though barely below a whisper. She saw that several people had their cell phones out, someone probably calling for an ambulance—or filming. They might have recorded the person who had pushed her.

The young man who had pulled her back from the street tried to steer her to a nearby bench, but all of a sudden, she couldn't handle being touched. She tore herself out of his grip even though the pain from various places made her eyes water.

"I'm fine!"

"Joanna!" She found herself face to face with a panicked Vanessa.

"It's not what you think," Joanna rushed to explain, now shaking in earnest which had little to do with the cold. "Someone pushed me."

"I know," Vanessa said grimly. "And I can describe him. We're going to the hospital first. I'll call Theo on the way."

"Can't I just go home…?"

Truth be told, Joanna didn't mind someone else taking over for a while as the ground beneath her became unsteady again.

"Whoa. I don't feel so good."

Chapter Twelve

S he would have liked to avoid the sympathetic looks of nurs-
es, and the police officer that came with Theo. Joanna knew
what they were thinking. She was lucky Vanessa had witnessed
the incident when waiting outside the bar for the cab to arrive,
even luckier she could describe the man. A couple of bystanders
had offered their phones, but nothing conclusive had come
from their recordings.

Was it Grace's boyfriend? Someone completely unrelated?
How many enemies had she made in the past years? Her head
hurt. Joanna didn't want to try and answer any more questions.
She would have preferred to be alone right now, but apparently
that was not an option.

"Think," Theo said. "Before or after you met Grace, were
there any threats?"

"I keep to myself, and I like to have a drink on a weekend
night," Joanna said. At the moment, it was of little relevance
how often she'd had more than one drink on a weekday. "That's
hardly threatening to anyone. Decker's widow moved away
right after the trial, and she never tried to contact me. Other
than that, I can't think of anyone who'd want me dead. How's
it going on your side? You really think Grace is going to make
bail?"

"I hope not," he said, shooting a quick resigned sideways glance at Vanessa who shrugged.

They were an odd kind of family, sharing everything, Joanna thought.

"Can I go home now?" she asked. "There's nothing else I can tell you."

Theo waited until the other officer was out of earshot, then he said, "I know you're both going to be mad at me in a second, but if it's not me, someone else is going to ask that question. How much did you have to drink tonight?" His tone was tinged with disappointment, though it was unclear if that went for Vanessa or Joanna.

"I saw the man clearly, and I told you so." Vanessa was furious. "What does that have to do with anything? Yes, we had a few drinks, now what? We didn't make the whole thing up! Hell, I really have other things to do with my life!"

Joanna assumed their earlier conversation about past regrets might have to do with her intense reaction. She, on the other hand, was almost used to being doubted. What did that mean?

"Enough," she said. "We had enough to drink. I could have just slipped, but we all know I didn't, and if the other people hadn't reacted this quickly, I wouldn't be here to talk to you."

Theo nodded. "All right. We'll find him and get ourselves some answers. Get the information out. I'll drive you home. Vanessa, you're coming with me?"

Vanessa followed without any further word.

The scene wasn't encouraging Joanna to try her luck with Rue, though somewhere deep down inside, she really wanted to. Perhaps being alone scared her more than involving Rue in some kind of imaginary or real danger...but it wasn't up to Joanna to make that decision for her.

Half an hour later, she stood in the bathroom, still feeling nauseated and chilled. No bones had been broken, she was lucky that way. Joanna didn't feel very lucky.

"Are you okay in there?"

Vanessa had insisted on coming with her. Joanna hoped she would go, and at the same time, she was scared of when she would.

"Peachy. You can go home now. It's Christmas Eve, for Christ's sake."

"Yeah, and why would I be there all alone? It's all right."

"You can't stay here," Joanna said, taking inventory of all the cuts and bruises from her encounter with concrete and solid ice. Judging from the picture, the concrete and ice had clearly won this round. Damn it. She wasn't going to cry. Not now, not again. "There's no space, and I'm not sharing a bed with you."

"Oh, I don't know, that armchair looks pretty comfortable."

"What is Theo saying about this?"

"Theo is working. He'll let me know as soon as they find the guy. You shouldn't be alone right now."

Joanna thought it was ridiculous, this conversation through the bathroom door. That made her want to cry even more. She was sure Theo and Vanessa had conspired together, and they didn't even think she could take care of herself.

"I'm going to smoke." That might work as a threat.

"No, you're not. Your bed is ready, and we're both going to get some sleep."

Joanna leaned against the door, deciding she had no more energy to fight the inevitable.

"Do what you want."

When she got out of the bathroom, she saw that Vanessa had indeed made the bed. The couch transformed into a small double bed, and despite Joanna's warnings, Vanessa had made herself comfortable on one side of it.

"Don't worry. I'm not going to get too close. Relax. Every-thing is going to be better tomorrow."

Joanna had no idea where her boundless optimism came from, but she didn't ask.

"Let's hope and pray," she said. "Good night."

For Grace, it was a Christmas miracle. The police wouldn't have the DNA results before the holidays. She'd make bail the moment she could get a hearing.

She was still furious, at Edward, at herself. How could she have not seen this coming?

What if she didn't make it out?

There was no doubt Edward would find another partner soon. He was charismatic and convincing when he wanted to be.

Where would that leave her?

And what if she gave him up?

Grace shook her head. There was no guarantee that the police would find him, and for sure, he wouldn't forget who had ratted him out. It was better to stick to the plan. Hopefully she could convince him to do one more before they got the hell out of Dodge. Yes, that one more. It mattered to her. After that, it was probably smart to take a break. She needed to come to terms with how Joanna had brushed her off, then only returned to try to get information out of her. Once she got her revenge, she'd be able to let go and leave.

Grace sighed.

If only the DNA results didn't come in...they were always careful, but they might have gotten a little carried away with Felicity at the killing site. If the cops had found it...She needed to get out of here within the next few hours. She hoped Edward would speed it up a bit. After all, she had given him so much in the past years.

❧

When Joanna woke, she was confused by the smell of coffee and food, even more so, when Kira came out of the kitchen a moment later.

"Good morning," she said. "I hope you're hungry. Merry Christmas."

"What...?"

"Your friend Vanessa called me, because we all know you'd be too proud to do it, and I'm glad she did. You shouldn't be alone right now."

"She's crazy," Joanna mumbled. "You have a family. It's Christmas."

"We are family too, remember?"

Joanna did remember. They had been there for each other during the long dreary days in prison. She didn't want to deepen the subject.

"In any case, we're okay. We did the gifts early this morning—it's not like the kids haven't been up since four-thirty or so—and I arrived before Vanessa left. You were dead to the world."

"That's not a pretty phrase."

"No, it's not," Kira agreed. "Come on, let's eat. She said they'd call you when they find the guy."

Joanna shrugged. "I'd feel better if they caught him...did she say anything else?" The deadline to keep Grace behind bars must be almost up. "I'm just going to make a quick call, okay?"

"Hurry up. The eggs are getting cold."

"Yeah." As she moved around the apartment, various pains made themselves known. Aware of Kira's gaze, she tried not to wince as she picked up her cell phone and chose Vanessa's number.

"Hey, it's me. I wanted to let you know there was no reason to take Kira away from her family today—but thank you—and if there's any news regarding Grace."

"Oh, there's news," Vanessa said triumphantly. "Good news. Grace is going to stay with us a little while longer."

"Great. Thank you."

Joanna finally joined Kira in the small kitchen, thinking the day was starting with gifts after all.

⁕

Kira had struggled for years with an abusive boyfriend who pinned his drug business on her when he was busted. She had worked hard to get back on her feet after the prison sentence and managed better than most. Thinking of her story, Joanna once again reflected that it might be time to count her own blessings. She had friends in unusual places that cared about her. They *were* her family.

"I didn't buy you a present," she said wistfully.

"I didn't think you had the time, hunting after serial killers and all." Kira's voice softened. "Don't you think it's time to let go?"

She had undoubtedly seen the printouts, as had Vanessa.

"Believe me, I was starting to see the wisdom in that. Then someone tried to throw me under the bus."

Kira looked troubled.

"This is exactly the reason why you should stay out of it. You don't have the resources you used to have."

"Well, I still own a gun, and sometimes I can guilt Theo or Vanessa into telling me things."

"That's not the same and you know it. I want you to be around, Joanna. Someday I might tell my kids how I made it through on the inside, and I want them to know who did that for me."

"Let's not talk about this now." Joanna sipped her coffee. "I want to enjoy the one time someone made breakfast for me. I really appreciate it."

"Promise," Kira insisted.

"What, to back out and let these guys do whatever the hell they want? What if the cop who busted your ex had this kind of attitude? Just let it go because you can't get them all anyway?"

"You're right," Kira said. "Let's not go there."

Chapter Thirteen

R ue sat on her living room couch, with the TV Christmas special running in the background, as she contemplated her options. She hadn't gone back to Mitchell's, instead written and sent her official resignation. There was no turning back. So far, none of the companies she was supposed to interview with, had contacted her with bad news, but it was the holidays.

She had told her parents earlier that she couldn't make it before the 27th, as she had to work over Christmas, but that was a moot point now. She wondered if she should change her plans, call them, and go. Rue hesitated. Her parents were middle class, had worked their way up to achieve their goals, which seemed modest in comparison to the opportunities Rue had. They would be worried to hear she had quit a well-paying job with no new one safely lined up yet, but she thought they would eventually understand she had to follow her conscience.

They had heard the occasional ignorant comments from neighbors regarding Rue, so they weren't strangers to blatant homophobia. She could probably explain herself, but that was part of the problem—she needed time to think, not dispute. She wanted answers from Joanna. For a moment, she fantasized about introducing Joanna to her parents, unsure how that would go.

They always had accepted her without conditions or any catch. Certainly, they would wonder about Joanna's story.

She jumped when her cell phone started vibrating on the glass coffee table, hoping it could be the woman who had occupied her thoughts almost 24/7 since their last, rather disastrous meeting. As it was, the message came with mixed news.

She remembered Vanessa from the night she'd first met Joanna, but what she had to tell Rue wasn't so reassuring.

"Oh my God," she said out loud. Her next thought, rather irrelevant given the circumstances, was that it was Christmas day. She shouldn't come empty-handed, right?

A plan was forming in her mind. She could still see her parents in two days, use the rest of the time to figure out what was really going on, with Joanna, between the two of them.

Rue packed a small overnight bag—too optimistic?—put on her coat and left her condo, mentally calculating which grocery store would by best to swing by on her way.

Halfway there, she shook her head to herself, laughing though the news made her feel more like crying. She had jumped at the chance to see Joanna again and hopefully help her out in a difficult situation, not even knowing if Joanna was interested in that help.

If that didn't give her all the answers, Rue didn't know what would.

Despite the dire occasion, she felt excited.

⁂

They had done the dishes together and settled in the living room. After another half hour, Kira looked at her watch with a sigh. "I'm sorry. I guess I have to go."

"Don't be sorry for that. I'm sure your folks are waiting for you. Thank you—for everything."

At the door, Kira hugged her, and Joanna tried not to wince.

"You're welcome. And remember what you promised, okay?"

Joanna didn't think she would feel like investigating or pursuing any difficult conversations today. Instead, she might go straight back to bed once Kira was out of the apartment. She had a lot to think about, but she wanted the conflicting voices to be silent for a little while.

The doorbell rang, which set off an instinctual reaction. She pulled Kira back into the apartment and put a finger to her lips. After last night, she had felt surprisingly safe in her home, but it was better to be safe than sorry. She didn't expect anyone at this time. Vanessa was still at work. Who else would come to see her? She didn't want to risk her friends' lives too.

"Who's there?"

"It's Rue. Are you going to let me in? I hope so because I brought food."

Joanna spun around to face Kira who shrugged.

"Don't look at me. I really need to go now. If you're looking for a suspect, I think Vanessa got her number from your cell phone. Just a theory. Bye, J."

"Yeah, sure, come on up," Joanna said, hitting the buzzer before she let Kira out. She waited in the hallway. Kira waved and turned for the stairs.

The manipulative tactics of her friends amazed her. Obviously, Vanessa felt like she had a lot to make up for. Then Joanna realized that she was wearing an old shirt and sweats and looking more than a little worse for wear. Did Rue know what happened? Was that why she was here? She had no more time to give these questions a lot of thought. She heard the sound of the elevator.

The doors opened and Rue stood in front of her with two grocery bags, her eyes widening when she looked at Joanna.

"I, uh, I'm so sorry about what happened. How are you doing?"

"Okay, I guess. You want to come in?"

"Yes. Sure. I thought we could put this away for now, and I'll make us something later. I imagine you don't feel like cooking much?"

Despite herself, Joanna had to laugh.

"That wouldn't be so different from any other day, but...Hey, I'd understand if this is too awkward for you, and you don't want to be here. I know Vanessa put you up to this, with or without Kira's help."

"I didn't need much convincing," Rue said softly as she walked inside. "I thought maybe we could be friends too—at least. Does that sound stupid? I have until the 27th. I promised my parents I would see them then. And I had a rather unpleasant conversation with your dad which convinced me to quit my job."

"Oh Rue. You shouldn't have done that."

Rue halted for a moment, obviously becoming aware she'd hardly taken a breath since she walked in.

"Don't worry, it wasn't as spontaneous and reckless as it might sound. Well, it's still kind of reckless. I have a couple of interviews next week. He wasn't happy though."

"Let's put this away, and then we can talk," Joanna said, unsure how to take this news from Rue. The last thing she'd wanted was to create trouble for her. After all, she still did care. "Wow. What is all this?"

"I wasn't sure what you had in the house. I wanted to make sure I had everything."

They worked silently, and after Joanna's fridge and tiny pantry were filled to the max, she led Rue into the living room.

"Okay. Now tell me what this is all about. I didn't mean you should quit the job, I'm sorry if it came across that way. It's not up to me, and...I overreacted. I'm sorry."

"I'm sorry too. I should have told you. But honestly, that's not even what it was all about. I knew a long time ago I had to leave certain things alone, that if I didn't, everything would come to the surface. Well, it did."

"I know how that feels."

She had made compromises and concessions when she was younger, but sins of omission got her only so far. When Lawrence confronted her about her sexuality and gave her an ultimatum, Joanna wasn't willing to gamble on her identity any longer.

"I know you do, and whatever he might do now, you gave up a lot more. I'll be okay. I'll find another job."

"What can he do?" This was odd, like talking about a malevolent stranger. Maybe it was her way of denial. She hadn't talked to her father in many years, and a part of her still wondered if she could have done anything to avoid this outcome.

"Not that much, I don't think so. Not everyone in town is queasy about hiring a lesbian, especially when that has nothing to do with the job...and I wouldn't want to work for one of his pals anyway, that wouldn't be much of a change."

"In that case...Congratulations?"

Rue laughed. "I'm not sure. I think so. Now tell me what happened to you."

⟨❧⟩

A young woman called the precinct in the late afternoon, claiming her neighbor, Marshall Stevens, looked exactly like the man who had pushed a woman in front of an oncoming bus the day before.

It turned out Stevens had been a nuisance to the whole apartment building, harassing the women, scaring the kids whenever he had the opportunity.

Now, Theo and his partner Allison were interrogating him, while Vanessa had stolen away from her desk to watch from behind the two-way mirror. This case interested her. Of course, everything about Joanna Mitchell interested her ever since she'd made the decision that changed both of their lives irreversibly, boosting her career and ending Joanna's.

Vanessa had felt guilty every day, more in the beginning, less so in the past year, but she still felt a sense of responsibility. The idea of a serial murderer coming after Joanna made her uneasy, mostly because she knew her friend wouldn't back away from the challenge.

That wasn't exactly fair. Killing Decker had been more than a challenge to Joanna. Vanessa was afraid there could be a confrontation with the slasher, and it could go either way. If this man turned out to be Grace Lester's partner—or vice versa—they could all consider themselves lucky.

Theo sat down across from the man, Allison remained standing.

Marshall Stevens looked nervous, doing a bad job trying to hide it. Under the table, he was tapping his foot on the linoleum floor, stopping whenever he realized it only to start over again. It drove Vanessa crazy, and she wasn't the one in the room with him. Or maybe it was an act trying to convince the police he hadn't murdered women across the country for years. Without a doubt, the killers would have skills that helped them to distract and blend in.

"You've had some time to think, Mr. Stevens," Theo said. "What's it going to be?"

"I didn't do nothing!" Stevens claimed. "It's freezing in here. This can't be legal."

Theo shrugged. "The heating is broken. Believe me, we're not happy about it either. Maintenance is on its way. So?"

"I don't even know the chick. Why would I want to kill her? Maybe she was drunk, wanted to blame it on someone."

Theo's gaze went to the mirror. Even though Vanessa knew he couldn't see her, the gesture uncomfortably reminded her of that night, the way people had initially doubted the story. Joanna had been on a downward spiral for a while, and maybe Vanessa didn't feel so guilty any longer, because she'd been there alongside with her, having drinks at The Copper Door often twice, three times a week.

Sure, an accident could have happened, but that wasn't the case here.

"There's just one problem. We have a witness who could identify you. She saw you push the woman. If no one had been there to help, we'd be investigating a homicide. How well do you know Grace Lester?"

"Who?"

The man's face turned a deeper shade of red.

"We know that you two met, and we know that she is friendly with a guy who likes to kill women, has done so for over a decade. You see where this is going?"

"This is crazy!" Stevens complained. "I didn't kill...I don't know anyone by the name of Grace Lester. You got the wrong guy."

"I don't think so." Theo tossed a photograph on the table. They'd pulled the image from the security camera of the apartment building. It was grainy, but both Stevens and Lester were identifiable.

Stevens looked like he was going to be sick.

"It was supposed to be a prank! And her name was Alice, not Grace. She said this other woman fucked her boyfriend, and she wanted me to scare her a little. She gave me a picture, and told me where to find her, and that's it."

"That's it? How much did she offer you?"

"One grand upfront and another after the deed. It looked to me like she had money."

"I'd say so." Theo and Allison exchanged a meaningful look.

Vanessa held her breath. She hadn't known they were this far into the investigation. Did that mean the nightmare was finally over, and Joanna could get rid of the stacks of papers in her apartment?

"You need some money if you want to order a hit."

"A hit?" Stevens laughed, though it didn't sound convincing. "A hit. You guys are funny. That's not what this was about, okay? She just wanted to get back at her."

"A thousand dollars for a prank? Are you sure you two didn't plan the whole thing together from the beginning—like the other murders?"

"Are you deaf or something? I keep telling you, I didn't kill anyone. She approached me in a bar, asked me if I wanted to make some quick money. Then she told me the story." When his words met with silence, he insisted, "I swear! You have to believe me, damn it, yes, I pushed her. There were lots of people who pulled her back before the bus was even close."

Liar, Vanessa thought, disgusted. The fact that Joanna had gotten away with some bruises was a matter of inches and seconds. It could have gone either way.

What troubled her even more was that other than this detail, she believed his story, and she sensed that Theo and Allison did too.

That meant Grace's real partner was still out there. She refused to give him up, and as for now, she planned on pleading not guilty. With only circumstantial evidence, and Christina's memory too sketchy for a damning testimony, a conviction didn't seem likely.

"That was Vanessa," Joanna said, surprised she was feeling slightly shaky. Yes, it had been a close call, but it wasn't the first time. "They found the guy. He confessed...But they don't think he's the killer. Well, at least one more unpleasant person off the street for now."

"That's good news though."

"Yes, it is." She sat back down next to Rue. "I think that's really my cue to take a step back."

"There are other things...in the future, and for now. For starters, I could cook you a nice Christmas dinner."

"It's still amazing to me that I'm the one who needs to apologize, yet you came to make me dinner."

"You apologized. It's all good." Rue hesitated. "Vanessa said you were going to be okay, but...This really gave me a scare."

"Yeah, tell me about it."

"Life is too short to keep wondering what other people think of you. It's too short to work for misogynistic, homophobic people when you don't have to. And...I realized that I almost lost you before I had the chance to get to know you. I know this sounds corny, but—"

"No, not at all. I know exactly what you mean. Why don't we...start over? Again?"

Rue looked intrigued, so Joanna carried through with the thought. "Hi, I'm Joanna. I killed a murderer once, and given the chance, I'd probably do it again, no matter the crap that happened afterwards. I work in a warehouse now."

"I'm Rue, and I used to work for your father. I have lots of remorse about that, but I quit, and now I'm between jobs...and hopefully, in a new relationship."

It was a moment on the edge of an emotion that could go anywhere, laughter, or something else. They leaned forward at the same time, eager for the warmth of the other's embrace. Eager for so much more, but there was a lot of time until Rue had to leave for her parents.

They cooked together, ate a meal by candlelight and took a hot shower together. They ended Christmas day making love carefully and slowly, given Joanna's condition. She could almost make herself believe that this was the start of a new life, without the monsters that had occupied the old one, the violence, the pain.

She was falling in love.

There was still a killer out there, but he was none of her business.

Right?

❦

Grace paced the length of her cell angrily, a small piece of paper crumbled in her right hand. She had read the words a million times, it felt like. They were burned into her mind now. What they meant, what they could mean. Everything depended on making the right decision now.

She had thought Edward had a plan, one that included getting her out. Now the cops had dangled Joanna in front of her like a prize far out of reach, and for all Grace knew, she might hook up with the girl from the bar again. Or another girl. She'd had friends once, who would help her without hesitation. Where were they now?

She couldn't believe it.

This wasn't a dream though. Her reality had shifted, in the form of these words hastily written on lined paper.

"Thank you for everything. We shall meet again someday."

He was dumping her.

It was too bad she didn't have a real lawyer at hand who could tell her if at this point, denial, or serving them Edward on a silver platter, would serve her better. She had to make a decision soon.

Chapter Fourteen

Joanna missed Rue the moment she walked out of the door, even though they had made plans for the night when she'd be back from her parents. Joanna hoped one of the job interviews would work out. Even though Rue had told her not to worry, she felt responsible for Rue's decision, partly at least.

She went back to work, trailing through her shift nearly on autopilot, thinking she should invite Vanessa and Kira over soon as well. For the first time, in a long time, she was moving forward. It was real. There was no point in always waiting for the other shoe to drop, was there? Old habits died hard, but there was nothing left to fear, for her, anyway. Christina had returned to her apartment and made arrangements to leave the city.

Grace would have her trial, those disastrous dates with a serial murderer nothing more than a faint memory.

Why couldn't she calm down?

During her break, she talked briefly to a colleague. He'd heard from Nate who was finally on vacation with his family. She wondered if the experience was still haunting him, even under palm trees. Joanna was fairly certain. The confrontation with what people were willing and ready to do to others, out of greed, for gratification, changed a person. You could never go back to the bliss of ignorance.

After her shift, she didn't feel like going out—there was nothing out there for her. There was no message from Rue. She probably didn't have the time yet.

The small rooms seemed to echo with memories. She was too melodramatic about this, Joanna was aware. They still didn't know each other well.

After coming out of the shower, she sat down on the side of the bed, remembering Rue's hands and lips, tender on her naked body.

The ghosts were gone.

It was a bit scary to think of a life without them. They were all Joanna had known for the past years. Her purpose had changed.

"I love you," she whispered.

One day, she would tell Rue the whole truth, the complete picture that not even Kira or Vanessa had seen. How she'd doubted her decision every day, how she had felt unbearably selfish for moments of wishing she'd let Decker go and kept her job and old life. The embarrassing reality of the first encounters with Grace.

The day she'd almost killed herself in prison, and that she owed Kira for still being alive.

She wouldn't burden Rue with those stories all at once. They had a lot of time, and Rue hadn't run yet, on the contrary. The future looked full of hope.

10 hours ago

Rue was deep in thought as she climbed into the cab getting her to the airport. The past days had gone by like a dream, some of it a tad unsettling, some of it so delightful she was almost afraid to jinx it. She didn't think Lawrence Mitchell could do her much harm—she knew from her everyday work that the two firms she had applied for had a different business philosophy, so she hoped for the best.

Then there was Joanna.

It might have been too quick, too easy, and they hadn't done much talking while enjoying each other's company.

Breathe, Rue told herself. There will be time.

She leaned back in her seat, glad that this was the one rare driver who didn't try to engage her in small talk. She'd spend a couple of days with her parents, catch up, then come back to pick up where she and Joanna had left off. She almost changed her mind, but she wanted to tell them the news before they, for some reason, might hear them from someone else. Joanna was right to be cautious—one could never tell how people would react to a story like hers. While Rue believed her parents would support her no matter what, she wanted some quiet time with them to explain all the changes she had made in her life lately.

She felt giddy. It wasn't like her life had been so bad as long as she had kept her mouth shut at her former job. She hadn't been unhappy as a single woman and had only signed up on the website to get her co-workers off her back. Some dates had been fun, some not so much...and eventually she'd walked into The Copper Door, readied herself for a disaster and found Joanna.

Rue was a firm believer in actions over words. While everything Joanna had told her rang true, she based her verdict on her instincts, the way Joanna acted around her, and the way she made her feel. Safe. Respected.

It made all the difference in the world.

She yawned, hoping the flight would be quiet so she could catch an hour or two of sleep. The rain outside would soon turn to ice. It better not impact the flight. Rue straightened in her seat, startled to see the unfamiliar surroundings. Was the cab driver daydreaming too?

"Excuse me? Sir? Where are you going?"

In the mirror, he gave her a smile.

"Don't worry, Ma'am. You're not going to miss your flight. I just have to make a stop on the way."

Rue wasn't at all assured. "Can't you do that later? I'm really in a hurry."

"Yeah, I bet."

His tone was level, but it still sounded like a sneer to her. Was she paranoid? Who was this man? Meeting Joanna, while a wondrous turn of events in the first place, had also opened her mind to all the horrible possibilities of what could happen. She had to take the damn cab to the airport, no way around it. Why did she have to end up with a weirdo?

"You know what, why don't you let me out at the next light, and I'll go from there?"

They were just barely out of the city limits. She could always take a chance and call another cab, hopefully finding a more responsible driver. To her surprise, he seemed unfazed by her suggestion.

"If that's what you want, lady, no problem. Why don't we stop right here?"

There were some industrial buildings spread alongside the road, and a parking lot. At this point, Rue didn't even know exactly where they were, but she was sure she wanted to get rid of this man. A cab driver could certainly identify the place by the name of the companies. She'd be fine.

She stepped outside in the freezing rain, cursing the man and her own bad luck. Hopefully she could get another car soon. She might miss that flight and get a cold on top of it...Joanna's chance to take care of her in return might come sooner than expected.

The driver came around to take her luggage out of the car, and predictably, he didn't care if they landed in a puddle.

"Hey, why don't you pay attention?" Rue shouted, frustrated beyond measure with her situation as she looked for a number on her phone.

She didn't quite know how it happened, but seconds later, she found herself face down on the ground, fear flooding her body and mind as he held her down.

"Don't talk to me like that, bitch!"

What was happening? She tried to remember the moves from a self-defense class taken years ago, to no avail. She was shaking too hard, from the cold, from the panic consuming her. Rue had read stories about cab drivers assaulting women—it was one of those things you knew happened, but you never thought it could happen to you. He pressed a damp, foul-smelling cloth against her face, and the world became a gray smudge turning black.

＊

While he couldn't help Grace, pity, he could at least fulfill her fantasy. No pleasure, no deceit for Rue—he didn't have that much time anyway. Just this one, and it would be time to return to warmer pastures. He had always known it was dangerous to come back here, with Joanna still around, and cops who remembered him. He had no interest in her any longer now that she'd become this pitiful story, no longer a hunter on equal footing with another. He felt obliged to Grace who had stood faithfully by him all those years, and truth be told, this one would be fun.

Above all he'd wanted to say hi to his elderly mother who thought he was a successful businessman in L.A.

From lawyer to cab driver, Edward was back to plain, mean serial killer.

Chapter Fifteen

A t ten to eleven, Joanna walked into the police station, seeking out Vanessa after she found Theo's desk empty.

"What gives? I called Theo and left him a message, but he didn't call me back. I'm worried about Rue. She didn't call me back and...hell, I know she's an adult and something probably came up, but I'd still feel better if he checked up on that." While she was talking, the expression on Vanessa's face told her already that there was news, and it wasn't good. "What? I know this isn't priority, but—"

"Joanna."

She forced herself to stop.

"It's priority now."

Just like that, the ground opened up under her. The possibilities were endless, right? Traffic, a minor accident, the plane canceled because of weather conditions...They could handle all of that. But it wasn't what Vanessa was talking about.

"Tell me," she said.

"Theo checked with the airport like you asked him. Her plane departed on time, but she wasn't on it. The cab company says they sent someone, but she never showed up."

"That's not true. I saw her get in the car."

"I don't doubt that. I haven't seen the driver that was supposed to pick her up, but he seems to be believable."

"So, we don't know anything for sure yet, right? It could be completely harmless."

Come on, humor me already. Rue was supposed to be on that plane, back home with her in a few days. It was still possible, wasn't it?

"Her cell phone is off. There's something else. Lester's lawyer disappeared all of a sudden, and we have reason to believe that he wasn't who he pretended to be."

Joanna couldn't believe what she'd just heard.

"You want to tell me the bastard walked in here and no one knew—"

"Actually, she's told you a lot more than you were supposed to know."

Neither of them had heard Theo come in. He looked tired.

"Joanna, you know we appreciate your contribution, but you need to step aside and let us do our job. We're going to find her."

"I don't doubt that," Joanna said, irritated with the implications of his words. "You know what to do, right? He kidnapped another woman without Grace. You need to lean harder on her. He has abandoned her. She might be willing to give him up."

"Yes, I know all that." There was a slight edge to his tone. "Now go home and wait until you hear from us. I'm not kidding."

"Let me do it," Joanna said. "Please. She was biding her time the other day, but I know I can get to her."

"Why do you think that?"

"He took Rue because of me. Grace knew from the beginning." Saying those words out loud made her sick to her stomach, but she couldn't deny the truth any longer. "She was jealous, sent me a lot of text messages, then they stopped all of a sudden around the time you found Felicity. They had to lay low, but they kept planning."

"It would be easier to just skip town, wouldn't it?"

"He has unfinished business. With me."

"Oh, for the love of—"

"Let's not waste any more time, okay?"

Joanna had hoped Theo would have a better idea, but he nodded.

"All right. Allison will go with you. See what you can do."

As long as she kept walking, doing something, she'd stay sane. She had gone over the old cases, and the new ones, in her mind so many times, the details were vivid. She couldn't stop for a moment and dwell. Christina had gotten away. They would find Rue before the slasher hurt her, and for sure, Joanna included herself in that. She wouldn't sit around idly, no matter what Theo said.

Allison gave her a quick nod, all business. Theo's partner since Joanna's arrest, she was the most uncomplicated cop and person Joanna had ever known. By the book, following all the rules, a bright career ahead. Joanna had envied her more than once, but today wasn't the time for such pettiness.

"You're back!" Grace clapped her hands in excitement. "I'm thinking you miss me. I miss you too. I often think about the nights we spent together."

"Yeah, me too." Worst sex of my life. Worst choice of my life. "Grace, why don't we put all the cards on the table now? We know that your boyfriend posed as your lawyer. He's taken off on his own, and he's going to make the kill without you. Why don't we spoil his fun?"

Grace gave her a long speculative look.

"You think there's still a 'we'? After you fucked that bitch? You betrayed me."

Each word was like a gut punch. It was hard to tell which was worse, had it been Grace's plan or the slasher's to go after Rue. Each theory opened another door to a world of horrors.

"Yes, I did. I'm sorry about that. I came here to apologize."

"Is this even legal? I mean, not only are you no longer a cop, but you're an ex-cop who executed a suspect. That's kind of...iffy, isn't it?"

"Don't worry about it. You're safe here," Allison interjected, her tone dripping with sarcasm. Grace ignored her.

"Well, they let me in here twice," Joanna reminded her. "Because I'm not a cop. You can believe me when I say prison is no fun. Except...if you tell us what we need to find him, you could still have some life on the outside left. If she dies, it's all on you."

"And you're going to do what, come to prison and kill me like you did with that Decker guy?"

I might, was the first instinctive and highly irrational thought Joanna wouldn't share in front of the detective.

"Doesn't it bother you the least bit how this is going to end? He gets to go on without you, and you're going away forever—after all you did for him? That's loyalty. I really don't get it why you were mad at me in the first place. You love him. You're going to take the fall for him. Wow."

"You don't understand."

"I'll admit to that. How you can still stand by him after he killed all these women, I don't understand. Maybe you can make me."

"There's just one problem, Joanna," Grace said coldly. "I told the cops I'm just as mad as they are that the lawyer disappeared into thin air. I don't know what his deal was, but now I have to make do with a public defender, a kid barely out of law school. I don't appreciate that."

"You know you won't make it far if you stick to that version."

"That's not your problem, is it?"

Allison gave her a pointed look, and Joanna got to her feet.

"There's something you still don't realize, Grace. Right now, the cops are your friends. *I* am your friend. Hell, even the crappy public defender is your friend, and you should listen to what everyone is saying. If you're smart about this, you'll start selling your story, and that could even be literally. I'm sure reporters will fall over their feet trying to get an exclusive. That offer is almost up. I'll go outside and have a coffee with the detective now, and when we come back, you will have made your choice, one way or another."

"Oh, you got your badge back now?" Grace asked sweetly. "Who did you sleep with for that?"

Joanna left the room without an answer, and Allison followed her.

On the other side of the door, she took a deep breath, trying to get her bearings. Her instincts had been true in something. From the first time she met her, Joanna had felt like Grace's presence drained her. Sure, many women worked on the side of patriarchy, some obliviously, some gleefully—but Grace made her sick. Most serial killers hated women for one ridiculous reason or another, because they hadn't talked to them or smiled at them, because they refused to have sex with them. To have a woman step in and help one of them, become one of them, was particularly disgusting.

And because of that woman, Rue was now in danger.

She became aware of Allison's gaze on her, almost jealous. There was some sort of sad joke in that. Allison had no reason whatsoever to envy her.

"She actually listens to you," Allison said. "You might have a shot."

"I hope so."

She knew Allison had been hired after the fact, so she didn't harbor the same mixed and complicated emotions toward Joanna as most of her other ex-colleagues did. In the present moment, she appreciated that.

"Could you get me that coffee? And take your time?"

"Theo is going to kill me, but yes. Anything you say will be recorded."

"Okay. Thank you."

"Where's your coffee?" Grace asked when Joanna stepped back into the room.

"Detective Kato is getting one for me. It's just the two of us now. You know, I can't seem to stay away. I'm too curious as to why someone who's obviously smart and resourceful would give her life for a man."

Grace sighed as if Joanna was testing her patience.

"You got it wrong. You think it's all for him, but it isn't. I mean, sure, I owe him, he taught me a lot of things after all, but I didn't just stand by. I did everything Edward did, and yes, it pisses me off I'm not there to finish off little Rue. By the way, I'll deny I said any of this once the real cop comes back, because even the public defender will know how to have your testimony thrown out."

"Sure, go ahead." Joanna had retreated into a bubble, a place without emotions, from where she could continue to poke and get results. Otherwise, her hands would be around Grace's throat. Her fingers twitched in her lap under the table.

"You think I was somehow coerced into this, but it's not true. I wanted it. I wanted to experience everything."

"Why?"

"Think about it, Joanna. Think hard. You know."

"I haven't got a clue."

"Killing. It's the only thing that makes us equal to men. Don't tell me you didn't feel the thrill when you blew away Decker. That doesn't make you some righteous avenger of women, it just makes you the killer, not the victim."

"Murdering women alongside of him"—*Edward*—"made you feel less like a victim?"

"It's all in the choices we make. I chose to be free."

"Well, you're not free now, are you?" Allison had returned with the two coffees. "He wins after all…unless you tell us where he is."

Grace shrugged. "I have no idea where he is, but maybe you could ask his mother. She's the only reason why he had to come here to this cold ass town instead of staying in the sun. Violet Short. She has a cottage somewhere out in the burbs. Once a year, we have to go and visit Mommy."

Wherever Allison went from here, Joanna would go with her. That much she knew for certain.

Chapter Sixteen

The sharp smell roused her from a deep heavy sleep. Instinctively, she tried to get away from it, the smell and consciousness. Rue knew whatever would happen next, it wouldn't be good. She wanted to withdraw, go back to the safe place of oblivion.

"You're with me now, good. I'm afraid we don't have so much time. I would be on my way, but I figured...I owe Grace this one."

She blinked, trying to make sense of her surroundings. It seemed like they were in some sort of attic. The icy rain was still coming down hard on the roof, and—the next thought crossed out all the others abruptly as she realized her hands were tied above her head to a wooden beam in the middle of the room. She was in her underwear.

"Please." She was shaking so hard it was difficult to bring out the words. "You could just let me go, and you'd have a head start. I don't know where we are. You'd be long gone before anyone finds me!"

Rue saw the camera on a tripod, a few feet away, her stomach lurching.

"Sorry, I can't," he said matter-of-factly. "I made a promise, you know? They are going to lock her away for the rest of her life. It's all I can do for her now."

"Maybe she doesn't want you to—" She broke off her sentence when he started to laugh.

"Oh, believe me, she wants me to. You were Grace's choice, not mine. Don't worry. We'll make this quick."

Rue flinched violently when he reached out and drew a number of random lines across her chest and thighs.

"You know, we usually have a pretty elaborate script. Maybe Joanna told you about it. Find a girl in a bar who's interested in walking on the wild side, spend the night together and then...oops," he said in a mocking tone. "Then they realize they shouldn't have done that. I thought you were too old, but she just couldn't get over you and Joanna. I figured what the hell. We've been here four months, and the police are too stupid to catch us, me, anyway, it's going to be all right." He put the cap on the marker and tossed it aside, then pinched her cheek. "You hear me? It's going to be all right. Now smile."

He stepped behind the camera and took a few pictures. "That's it for now." He went to a space behind her.

Rue frantically craned her neck to find out what he was doing, seeing for the first time the table with the assortment of knives.

"No. Please don't."

Tears blurred the picture as he turned away from the table and disappeared down narrow steps to a lower floor.

Rue yanked at the ropes that bound her to the beam, but they didn't give.

Only minutes later, the smell of onions frying in a pan wafted up to her, and she started to sob.

Joanna had to be worried about the lack of communication by now. She had found and killed a murderer once.

On the other hand, if he was making a meal for himself, she had a few minutes to try and loosen these restraints, and maybe she could get to one of those knives—before he could...

Rue tried to push from her mind that the man Joanna had killed had already murdered those four women, and others before. Mila had gotten away from Decker. Christina escaped the serial murderer duo.

She had to be lucky too.

Tears were streaming down her face as she worked on the rope.

Allison hadn't even tried to keep Joanna from joining her, but she insisted on her wearing a vest. There was a chance Edward's mother was hiding her son, and in that case, she might be armed too.

Given how easily Grace had given up the location in the end, it could be a trap. Before the cops went inside the house, Allison came over to where Joanna had parked behind her on the curb.

"You stay in your car. Under no circumstances you get involved, do you hear me?"

"Clearly. I know the drill."

"Good. I understand what this means to you, but that's all the slack I can cut you."

"I understand. I'll stay here."

Allison, Theo and her colleagues had parked at a distance.

Joanna hated to be the one left behind, but as long as the horror ended here and now, she could live with it.

Violet Short was the mother to Edward Short, the man who had pretended to be Grace's lawyer, using a different name. With the security camera recording him during his visits with Grace, it had been easy to connect the dots.

Short had graduated from the local university and moved to California for a tech job, then began to do freelance work within the L.A. County but returned on occasion to visit Violet.

There was no doubt that the timeline of the murders would add up with travels Short had made. If he wasn't there with his mother, she might have an idea where he was, and she had better come up with an answer soon.

Leaning forward, Joanna tried to find a space in herself where she could escape from both the flashbacks and the present fear. She felt selfish for the attempt, as long as Rue was still in danger. Rue had nowhere to go.

Like Allison said, she had helped them, and they had cut her some slack in return. It didn't mean that door was open for her. One mistake, and they might lock her up too—again. But it didn't mean anything, nothing meant anything if she could never see Rue again.

Joanna unlocked the door and stepped out of the car.

❧

Maybe the rope was budging just a little, maybe it was all her wishful thinking. The smell of food from downstairs, both tantalizing and sickening to Rue, presented a jarring contrast to the nightmare she was trapped in. The skin of her wrists had to be raw about now, but she barely felt the pain, shuddering with each breath even though it wasn't all cold in the room.

Time.

Her friend, her enemy.

He might open a beer or two with his meal, fall asleep...or the alcohol would unleash another, worse beast. In the end, did it matter? Would she survive to tell her story, and if she didn't...Rue realized she was wondering about a possible afterlife, and if any of her experiences in life, good or bad, would be reflected.

She tore at the rope, only to have the pain kick in full force, bringing new tears to her eyes. It didn't matter. It was too early to think about the after, or even what the next few minutes.

Time.

It was all she had, and for the moment, all she had to fear.

"You can't go in here," the officer warned. Theo exited the building at this moment. Lucky for Joanna or not, it was still debatable.

"Did you find him?" she demanded.

He shook his head, apparently too frustrated with the outcome to chastise her.

"The house is clear. She identified him from the security camera photo, confirmed that he comes to visit every few months, but she has no idea where he is now. She seems horrified."

"A normal person would be. What now?"

"Joanna. We have a job to do here, remember? You're supposed to be home, or at work, whatever."

"He's going to kill her. There's no need for an elaborate ritual now, it's just to make a point."

Her eyes filled with tears. Joanna hated this, her own weakness, losing once again.

Losing Rue.

Decker had wanted to make a point with her too, by shooting the women Mila had befriended. Right here and now, Joanna couldn't help wondering if he had won after all. Killing him had done nothing to the finality of the deaths he'd caused.

She forcibly pushed her emotions aside, focusing on the next steps even though they weren't hers to follow.

"You should leave someone with her in case..."

"Yes. Allison will stay with her, though we think it's unlikely he'll come back. He visited last week, that was when he was still playing the lawyer. He only ever stays for one afternoon at a time."

"Can I?"

"Now you're asking?"

"You need to go."

"Don't do anything stupid," he said and turned for his car.

***

"What do you want?" Violet Short asked bitterly when she opened the door to Joanna. "I already had my house turned upside down by the cops. I didn't know the vultures would follow suit."

"I'm not a reporter, or a cop."

"What are you, then?"

"I'd say she's a nuisance following me around," Allison commented from the doorway. "Mrs. Short, I'm sorry, but could we go back to where we were before? Any little detail you remember could be important."

It was still unclear whether or not Joanna was invited to the table. She took the chance following the two women into the living room stuffed with old-fashioned furniture.

She could smell the dust, a cough tickling her throat. The wallpaper was something out of the seventies. Time had slowed down in here.

"What I remember is the son I once had, who made something out of himself, founded a business. A good man who never forgot his mother, or where he came from. Now you're telling me he's a murderer?"

Joanna could see a hint of impatience in Allison's expression, mirroring her own. Violet Short's life had been turned upside down, but another woman was about to lose hers.

Nothing was ever fair.

"True," she said. "That's exactly what we're telling you. I understand this is hard for you, but it is too for the families of the victims who have been waiting for eleven years. I've been waiting for eleven years. We need to end this."

"I can't help you! I don't have any property other than this house. Edward didn't even give me his new address in California, and for sure I didn't know he was living with a woman here."

"Do you remember any problems he might have had with girls when he was younger? In high school maybe?"

Behind Short's back, Allison was rolling her eyes, but she didn't say anything.

Men like Edward didn't just one day decide to go on a killing spree. They harbored a deep hate against people, mostly women, they felt owed them. They killed as a punishment, as a confirmation, anything to uphold their skewed version of reality in which everyone should always bow to them.

"The usual pranks, what do you expect? Boys will be boys, right?"

Joanna imagined herself getting up and shaking the woman, screaming at her that this was a lie that had made it possible for Edward and others to become predators. She did nothing of the kind, just listened, calm on the outside, terrified on the inside.

"What kind of pranks?" Allison asked.

"The principal once sent him home, because he'd been sneaking glimpses at girls in the locker room of the gym. That's a healthy interest to have, don't you think?"

It was a sign of a lack of respect for those girls' boundaries, but Joanna wasn't going to argue the point with Short now.

"Tell us more," she said. "Do you remember any names?"

Chapter
Seventeen

There were footsteps on the narrow stairs. Rue didn't have much time for the fantasy of someone—Joanna—coming to her rescue.

He was back.

The rope around her wrists had loosened some. It wasn't just her imagination. But it was too late. He went back to the table and picked up a smaller steak knife.

"You know," he said conversationally, "I said this was going to be quick, but we can't really end it before midnight. Grace always had this idea about having rituals, like real serial killers, so they'd put a profiler on the case and all that shit. Every kill tells a story, she said. Me, on the other hand, I just like stuck up bitches to get what's coming to them, but let's humor her, okay?"

Rue didn't think he expected an answer from her. In any case, her mind was racing too much to settle on any thought, her heart about to beat out of her chest. She flinched at the pitiful whimper escaping her lips as he moved closer.

He traced the point of the blade across one of the smaller lines, then applied pressure.

Rue gasped.

"Okay, let's do this," he said and chose another line. This time, she screamed.

Fear, adrenaline and the smell of onions and alcohol broke her endurance, and she threw up.

"It's Christmas," Detective Allison Kato reminded her. "People are with their families now, the school is closed."

Violet could give them the name of the principal at the time, but not much else. It was no surprise that Joanna wasn't satisfied with the information, or the pace of the investigation.

"You're just going to do nothing?"

"I didn't say that. Let's see if we can find that lady."

Allison picked up her phone and headed for the kitchen, holding up a hand when Joanna moved to follow her.

"You stay here."

To her surprise, Joanna complied. She was obviously near her breaking point, but Allison couldn't worry about her now. Like everyone else, she was painfully aware that a woman's life was at stake. She conducted a quick search on her phone, found the number and called it.

It took four rings before someone picked up.

"Hello?"

"Am I speaking to Marion Pyland? I'm Detective Allison Kato. I need to ask you about your time as principal in West Haven High."

Silence.

Allison could sympathize with Joanna's impatience. "Mrs. Pyland, are you still there?"

"Yes. What's so important you need to know on Christmas? It's been a long time since anyone has asked me about West Haven."

"I'm sorry about the inconvenience, but I need to ask you now. Do you remember an incident involving a student named Edward Short spying on—"

"Now, how old do you think I am? Of course, I remember Edward. Arrogant, that one, and his mother wasn't much of a help. Asked me if I'd prefer him looking in on guys. Why?"

"Mrs. Pyland, do you remember the names of the girls he targeted?"

"A couple, but I would have to look up the others. There are records at the school. You'd have to ask the new principal."

"Could you give me the name?"

"I certainly could, but is it really this urgent? You're lucky I'm alone, but she is probably with family..."

"Short abducted a woman, so yes, it is that urgent."

Mrs. Pyland gave her answers quickly after that. Allison returned to the living room where Joanna was pacing.

"Okay, this is what we have. She gave me the name of the woman who has the job now, and two names of girls he spied on. For the other names, we'll have to get the records from the school."

"What are we waiting for? We need to contact the new principal and go there right now!"

"Joanna, take a breath! Even if she gave them to us without a warrant, we have to find her first. She might be with family. I'll get the warrant and send a couple of uniforms to her house."

Allison Kato made several calls. At the department, one of their colleagues would run the names against those of the slasher's victims and find out if any of them still lived in the area.

"I'll have someone come over to your house," she said to Mrs. Short. "Joanna? Once they're here, I'll head over to the school."

"What were the names she gave you?" Joanna asked.

Allison saw no harm in sharing them.

Rue couldn't stop crying, and part of her was irrationally ashamed. The cuts had been superficial so far, mostly, not more painful than what she had done to her wrists all by herself.

Of course, it wasn't about that, but about the violation, body and mind. The man did it so casually, as if it was a mere task he had to fulfill, but she knew better. She knew every step excited him a bit more, fueled his sick thirst for blood.

She knew the next time he came back, he would go for the bigger knife, her stomach clenching at the thought.

Rue finally managed to pull her wrists out of the rope, nearly falling face first onto the floor.

He hadn't bothered to clean up. Why would he, when he planned to spill a lot more of her blood?

There was nothing in here to cover herself with. Could she risk going down, or would he be waiting for her on the bottom of the stairs?

Rue chose the biggest knife from the table, barely able to pick it up in a shaking hand. She reconsidered and took a smaller one.

If she was lucky, she never had to use it.

If she wasn't...who knew.

Principal Banks had no problem leaving her family dinner to join them at the school.

"What a terrible story," she said. "Yes, Mrs. Pyland told me about this once. A few of the girls filed reports with her, and I think he was suspended for a while, but there wasn't much else she could do. If only we knew what we know now, right?"

Boys will be boys. Harmless pranks. Upon a closer look, a different story was unfolding, a history of harassment and stalking. Joanna managed to take a look at the list of names.

"Okay. We'll get back to the station now and check up on those. Joanna?"

"Yeah. Sure."

Allison gave her a strange look, but she didn't comment.

Joanna got into her car, lost in thought.

It took her only a second to come up with the connection, even though her fear for Rue occupied her mind. One of those names rang a loud bell. Joanna made a U-turn that could have become dangerous if it wasn't a holiday night that left the streets empty.

Marcia Ellmers was the sister of a student Joanna had interviewed as a possible witness, eleven years ago. The memory came back to her so clearly because it had been one of the first interviews in that case.

No one connected the man seen near the killing place with a teenage boy who had spied on Marcia and other girls in the locker room years ago.

Until now.

Her sister Claire had seen a man in a track suit running down the path, and she thought there might have been blood on it. She and her friend, walking back to her parents' house, had been spooked and hid, but they could describe him somewhat.

It was back then that Joanna had hoped it could be days, not years before they caught him. The Ellmers family was still around, the daughters living in town as well. There might be a chance that they were all together for Christmas, at the family home.

Joanna remembered the area where it stood, not so far from where Decker had holed up in a cabin. Houses stood far apart, built with mostly wood. The snow had intensified now, and she could barely see a few feet ahead.

Was any of this making sense?

Should she get Theo or Allison, or would her theories pull valuable resources away from the investigation? What if the connection to the Ellmers family was a simple coincidence? The insecurity gnawed at her, but Joanna didn't think that talking to the Ellmers' would do any harm. If anything, she could save time for the investigators. They were following all leads right now. The family possibly remembered her too, the time she'd come by to take Claire's statement. If they had anything important to contribute, if Claire and Marcia could give any additional information regarding what Claire had seen, and what Short did in the girls' locker room that time, Joanna would pass it on right away. If her trip was futile, she wouldn't take up valuable time that might help save Rue's life.

Maybe she was going on a wild goose chase, because she couldn't bear the thought that for Rue, it might already be too late, even if Theo and Allison got to Short soon.

The place where the slasher's, Edward Short's, first victim had been found, didn't exist anymore. She drove past the area where Claire Ellmers had seen him run, all those years ago.

The Ellmers' house was a bit further down the hill, and she had trouble controlling the car on the icy dirt road. There was smoke coming from the chimney.

Joanna backed up a little until the car was hidden behind a row of trees and stopped. The wheels were in motion, and she had made a choice, to contribute whatever she could.

She might be lucky. Theo and Allison might have already found Rue, alive and unharmed. The story didn't always have to end the same, just because she was in it.

Joanna exited the car, intent on ruining a good family's Christmas vacation by bringing up a painful past.

A moment later, she could hear breaking glass, and screams.

Joanna turned around and got her gun out of the glove compartment before she hastened to the front door.

Rue had made it down the narrow stairs, miraculously without falling or dropping the knife. On this floor, there was a living area and a kitchen, two doors likely to lead to the bathroom and bedrooms. The man who had taken her was nowhere to be seen.

Now what? Where were her clothes? It was pitch dark outside, the snowstorm howling menacingly. If she went outside there now, she'd freeze to death. There was nowhere to hide...

She never saw him coming, but when he pushed her to the floor, Rue used the only chance she had and made sure the knife sank into skin and muscle. It wasn't just the storm howling anymore.

Theo was worried about the lack of contact from Joanna, but at least he knew she could take care of herself if necessary. Besides, he was too busy to deal with her now, with the clues coming together and their team closing in on Short.

He saw that Vanessa had tried to reach him and made a mental note to call her back later.

They had received a call from a former client of Short's who said Short had worked on his computer system for two weeks earlier this year and came by for his check just the day before. Theo went to see him while Allison followed up on the records the principal of West Haven High had provided her with. Only a few of the girls targeted back then, now grown women, still lived in the area. They would talk to all of them. Edward Short wouldn't get out of the city. Not this time.

Chapter Eighteen

There was blood on the hardwood floor. The vision and smell hit Joanna in a way she should have expected, but didn't, making her waver for a moment. Rue had ducked next to the fireplace, a dubious shelter.

Wood panels, hardwood floor, damn wood all around, reeking of copper and death.

Not again.

Short was bleeding, injured from a stab wound in his abdomen. He was standing up, wobbling on his feet, clearly intending to hurt her. Could he, still?

Joanna didn't wait. She pulled the trigger, twice.

The sound was deafening in the confines of the small building. Short toppled backwards, clutching his chest as he fell. Joanna ran over to him, confirming that he was unconscious before she turned to Rue. Her eyelids were fluttering, but her pulse was strong, no life-threatening injuries as far as Joanna could tell. Her skin was cold though, and she was clearly in shock.

She was alive.

"All right, let's warm you up first." Joanna took off her coat, carefully helped Rue to sit up, and wrapped it around her heaving shoulders. "We'll find something better in a second, I promise. Can you make it to that couch?"

The dishes on the table indicated this was where Short had enjoyed a meal with a few beers. She kept an eye on him, just in case, but there was no movement. Reluctant to let go, Joanna found a comforter to cover Rue with, then opened drawers and cabinets to find some clean towels she used to wash and cover the superficial wounds. She didn't get much of a reaction from Rue other than a pained moan. Joanna knew she had to call an ambulance, even though it would take them a while to get here in this weather.

For Rue.

She went back to Short's motionless body and checked for a pulse, startled when she found none. She couldn't find it in herself to worry about this now.

Joanna went back to the couch and leaned in close to brush a strand of hair away from Rue's face, satisfied that her temperature was getting better, and kissed her forehead softly.

"You'll be okay. I promise."

Then she made the call.

⚬

There was not a question in Vanessa's mind about what to do when she listened to Joanna relate the recent events. She was in her car an instant later, on the road. Theo hadn't answered her call yet, which was just as well. He would ask uncomfortable questions later, but she would deal with them, somehow.

She was driving too fast, lucky that there weren't many cars on the road. Many were still on their winter vacation and staying inside during this weather. She thanked God for four-wheel drive, and the brake check she'd gone for just a week ago.

Her truck came to a halt next to an unfamiliar car, and she ran the last steps to the house, nearly falling on the slippery steps.

Vanessa tried hard not to find the scene disheartening. On the contrary, Joanna was well and alive, Rue was...alive, and by whatever miracle they had to be grateful for, her life wasn't in danger, not anymore.

Edward Short was dead, and this was where it got complicated.

It was clearly deliberation on Joanna's part to call her, because they both knew, this time it would be someone else picking up the clues. They would see the similarities.

"I had to," Joanna said the moment Vanessa rushed into the room. "You have to believe me. I had no choice!" She was cradling Rue in her arms on the leather couch.

Somehow, she'd always known it would come to this moment, inevitably, at some point in their lives, and she'd be forced to make a decision that would be much harder than the first time. Joanna had crossed a line long ago, and she wasn't going back. If anything, the circumstances, and the people involved in this case, wouldn't let her.

"What about the family?"

"They weren't here. I checked quickly. I called an ambulance," Joanna said. "The dispatch officer said they'd be here as soon as possible, but there was a pile-up on the highway. We might be faster to drive her to the hospital."

"What about Short?"

"What about him? He has a table with knives upstairs. I couldn't just stand by."

She straightened, the color draining from her face. "You know what he did. Even if another widow with a crying baby appears out of nowhere, doesn't mean it didn't happen. Look at her!"

Rue flinched at the raised tone of her voice.

Vanessa had flinched too.

"He was going to kill her. I couldn't let that happen."

"I know. This is what we're going to do. Give me the gun."

"What are you—"

"Do it already!" Vanessa took a deep breath. "No, wait. Wipe it clean first, then give it to me. She'll have my coat. I bring the truck closer to the house, and I'll get her to the hospital." She could tell that Joanna wasn't entirely on board with the plan. "See if you find some clothes around here. Boots would be good. None of yours. If we're lucky, your DNA isn't all over the place, but as you know, that will take a while anyway."

"What are you saying?"

"You go to Kira's. Wait there until I contact you. I'm warning you, Joanna, this is a one-time thing, and it's off the moment you open your mouth to say no. I'm offering you a chance not to go back to prison."

Joanna's haunted gaze made her shiver. She had tried to make time for visits on a regular basis, but she remembered the one time she'd been turned away, when Joanna refused to see anyone, staying at the infirmary for a reason she and Vanessa had never talked about.

"I can't go back," Joanna said, which seemed more like an apology for Rue.

"I know. Now let's move. Rue will be okay, I'll see to that, but she should be in a hospital. She'll need more care than bandages on those cuts."

"I agree. Vanessa...thank you."

"Don't thank me yet. We still have a long way to go."

❧

When the time came, it still seemed unbearable to let go, and once again Joanna was asking herself if she did something self-ish, or the right thing. She had no illusion of what would happen if the authorities other than Inspector Young found out another murderer had died because of her.

It wasn't that there were many people to mourn these men—except for Decker's wife and Violet Short, maybe—but it was a matter of principle. At least, that's how Vanessa had explained it back then, when she'd been on the witness stand.

Now Vanessa had become an accomplice, helping her escape from a predicament that would have been likely to take her back behind locked doors. She doubted Rue remembered much of what had happened since Joanna entered the house.

Kira was waiting by the door, pulling her into a close embrace, and Joanna nearly lost it.

"Vanessa will arrange something. You don't ask any questions. You don't know anything."

"It's okay, sweetie. I got you. I'm glad we get to help."

"You're doing more than anyone has the right to ask for," Joanna said, choking up.

"You didn't ask for anything. Rue is going to be okay, thanks to you. You will be too."

"Maybe," she admitted. "But I can never see her again."

Rue came to with a scream, in a darkened hospital room. She was shaking and crying before she could even make sense of the situation but managed to breathe once she recognized Joanna's friend Vanessa.

Why wasn't Joanna here?

Had anyone notified her? Did she even know? Fear flooded her mind once more—and shame, irrational but inescapable.

"I know you probably have a lot of questions," Vanessa said softly. "The most important thing is that you are safe right now."

The memory came back to her in fragments.

Sharp edges.

Blood.

"They found your cell phone and luggage. From there, it wasn't far."

That didn't make sense. Then again, nothing had since the moment she'd realized the man in the cab wasn't a taxi driver.

"What day is it?" she croaked out. "I have a job interview... My parents..."

"They are on their way here."

Rue closed her eyes. She didn't want them here now, with their own questions and fears she didn't know how to answer.

"I'm sure you'll be able to reschedule that interview," Vanessa continued.

"Yeah. Maybe." There was no more escape. "What about Joanna? Is she...is she okay?"

"Joanna can't be here right now, but...I swear, I'm telling the truth. She's okay. Everything will be okay."

It wasn't enough of a satisfying explanation, but the drugs in her system pulled her back into sleep. She'd get her answers next time—and hopefully, Joanna would be here.

Chapter
Nineteen

V anessa's call, less than forty-eight hours later, only lasted about a minute. She gave Joanna instructions where to go, not to tell Kira in case the police questioned her, and said that Rue was doing well, considering.

"You hear me? Do not take any detours. You go there right away. Everything will be ready."

She ended the call before Joanna could answer, possibly to avoid an answer she wouldn't like. She shouldn't have mentioned the interview then. They might not have a future any longer, but there was something she could do for Rue. If it did any good was to be determined. Joanna couldn't jump ship without trying.

She and Kira hadn't talked much in those past hours. There was no need to reminisce out loud when the perimeters of their relationship had always been so obvious.

Back then, in prison, Kira was careful, staying under the radar, never missing work or a class. One day, she had attracted the wrong person's attention. Lucky for her, Joanna had been there when said person came after her with a knife that day.

At first, Joanna thought the subsequent solitary confinement didn't bother her so much. She didn't scream and rage, had in fact expected this outcome. At least, it was calm, much calmer than the block...and too much time to think, to study the images on the walls of her subconscious in depth.

Too many abused and dead women. She might have kept Decker from going on, but others would emerge, an endless cycle of entitlement and violence. Her actions had amounted to nothing, or at least it felt that way. When she was allowed back into her cell, Joanna started to withdraw. Maybe she had even made plans, it was hard to remember now, but she clearly remembered the feeling of being of no use to anyone.

Joanna remembered dreaming about that knife.

It was Kira who stepped in before she could lose herself in a place from which she could never return, and now, once again, Kira risked the life she'd built to help her.

"It's okay. Everything will be fine," she said as they sat together on her couch.

Joanna had a faint memory from when her mother had still been around, holding her, stroking her hair like that. It had been a lie back then. It could still be in the present.

No one could tell right now.

Regardless, there was something she needed to do.

⁕

Lawrence Mitchell looked up from his desk, slightly startled at the sight of his visitor.

"That's a surprise. I imagine you're in some kind of trouble. Again. My answer is still the same."

Joanna pushed the cutting disappointment aside. She had no time for it.

"I didn't come to ask you for money."

That was another point, come to think of it. Vanessa had a plan, obviously, including finances. Joanna wasn't yet sure what it was.

"That's...interesting. I'm working, as you can see, so..."

They hadn't talked in over a decade, and he couldn't get her out of his office soon enough. That was just as well, because she'd be happy to leave.

"I know you have the power to sabotage Rue's career. One word of advice, *Dad*...don't."

He gave her an amused smile.

"Or else you're going to shoot me? It seems like that's your answer to everything."

"How about doing the right thing for once? She's been through something horrible you can't even imagine. She doesn't need you messing with her life any more."

"I don't know what she told you, or what you're imagining, but no one is sabotaging her career. She knows I have friends in the business, and what our views are. We might be old-fashioned, but those are still family businesses."

"Yeah, sure, because living an authentic life is the worst a person can do in your eyes, and they must be punished...regardless of whether they were nearly murdered."

Pointless. She should have never come. He was probably going to call the cops. Vanessa would be mad.

"Murdered? What the hell are you talking about? Just look at yourself," he scoffed, shaking his head. "This is what you call an authentic life? Grow up, Joanna, and take responsibility. Then, maybe someday, we can talk. You can tell the same to Rue. I really liked her, but she was too stubborn, poking her nose in places she had no business. I know what you want to say, the world is changing and all...Well, I still think it's wrong. I am not changing."

"Okay, you made your point. I hope you remember mine. Good night, Lawrence."

"Wait! You won't tell me what's going on?"

"Why would I? You're not interested," she said. "That's fine. I came here because of Rue."

Perhaps that wasn't the whole truth. He didn't react to that, so Joanna left, finally heading to the place Vanessa had told her to go.

She found money, clothes, a burner phone and a note with a name and number on a piece of paper. *Call him. He'll take care of the rest.*

His work often came with messy situations. Theo preferred to end cases clean and neat, all loose ends tied up, an immaculate report that left no open questions, with as much detail as possible.

Prosecutors loved him for it.

Vanessa had told him it made her work easier too.

You could say that since the Decker "incident," he had even become a little more OCD about the process. Both he and Vanessa believed that there were certain rules for cops no one should ever break, because it would jeopardize the system as a whole.

Sitting at his desk, trying to make sense of what had happened, he was at a loss.

He needed to talk to Vanessa, get more information out of her than the vague description she had given him of the events. She had barely left Rue's bedside and driven her home after she was released from the hospital. She was with her now.

He needed to get a hold of Joanna, but she had vanished since those last calls to Vanessa, hadn't shown up for work in days.

Theo knew she had long been estranged from her father. It was worth a try though. He had exhausted all other angles.

On the surface, it was a satisfying outcome. Rue was alive. She didn't remember much after being drugged in a parking lot where Short had dumped her suitcase and cell phone.

Grace had confessed.

Edward Short was dead, two shots fired, prints of both Vanessa and Rue on the otherwise clean weapon. There were some things that didn't add up.

According to Vanessa, Joanna had a suspicion about the Ellmers house, but she wasn't certain, didn't want to bother the detectives with information that might lead nowhere.

In Theo's experience, Joanna wasn't shy about going after a hunch, or asking her former colleagues to do so if she thought it was important. He was almost certain she had been at the house, but if that was the case, why hadn't Vanessa told him?

She had gone there to do Joanna a favor, found Short standing over Rue. At some point, Rue seemed to have gotten hold of the weapon, but he'd taken it from her. She stabbed him with one of the knives laid out in a creepy line-up in the attic, blades that no doubt would match the injuries of the other victims.

However, when Vanessa came in through the unlocked door, the gun was on the floor. She admitted she'd picked it up and taken the shots rather than go for her own service weapon. Rue was bleeding. Vanessa had tended to her first and then called 911. Since the pile-up on the highway required lots of personnel, and Rue's injuries weren't life-threatening, she had driven her to the hospital. Short was already dead.

If Rue had managed to turn the tables on Short, good for her. He was worried about her, though, and Vanessa, too. It wasn't like her to go off by herself like this, and there would be consequences. Why hadn't she used her own weapon? Vanessa always kept a clear head under fire. What had she been thinking? Who was she protecting? And what if she'd actually done it?

Killing somebody weighed on a person, even if there was no other choice, and that person was a monster.

Where the hell was Joanna and why wasn't she by Rue's bedside?

⁕

Rue felt lost like never before in her life. Her parents were still in town, and she couldn't bring herself to ask them to leave. She didn't know how to handle Vanessa, who kept close for some reason. Part of her feared that she had bad news regarding Joanna and was waiting for Rue to be more stable before she shared it. The problem was Rue wasn't sure if stability was something she could achieve, anytime soon, or ever.

People—mostly Vanessa—kept telling her she was safe, and rationally she knew it was true. Grace Lester, who had wanted her dead out of jealousy, would be in prison for life. Edward Short, the man with the knives, was gone.

Feeling safe was a different story when there were too many shadows, too many facts uncertain. Vanessa said they'd talk soon.

If Joanna had simply lost interest, it would be the easier reality to accept.

The time with her seemed like a dream too, a treacherous illusion of hope. Rue didn't have much hope at the moment. She was busy trying to survive one day at a time, without panicking.

One of the firms she had applied for had expressed their regret of what happened and rescheduled her interview, even offered her part-time employment if she preferred.

Rue would have preferred to turn back time to a moment when she could have delayed the flight, stayed with Joanna instead.

The police might have caught Short.

The two of them would be...where?

Chapter Twenty

"You didn't shoot Short, and neither did Rue," Theo said after taking a seat on the barstool next to Vanessa, at The Copper Door. "I can't prove it, but I know it."

He wasn't sure whether Vanessa wanted to start a new tradition between the two of them, or if she was missing Joanna. In any case, she was on her second Martini.

"You know it because you're a good cop," she said. "The kind I never had to worry about before."

He ordered bourbon and waited until Jeff, the bartender, was out of earshot.

"Are you worried now?"

Vanessa didn't answer, instead stared straight ahead into the clear fluid in her glass.

"Do you ever wonder if what we think is right, really is?"

"Wow. That's deep. Do you know where Joanna is?"

She sighed. "Before you ask any more questions, you should know I don't want you to get into any kind of trouble. I'm not exactly sure where she is right now, and that's the truth."

He took a sip of his drink.

"It's not like Joanna to send you to check out a lead. When she found out that Short had taken Rue...that hit her hard. And she doesn't give up, ever."

"Joanna thought it was better not to bother you, and wasn't she right? Perhaps it's time for her to find some peace. Which hopefully means I can too."

It was Theo's turn to be silent, to weigh the odds and dangers of what to say next.

"When the test results are all in, we'll learn that Joanna was in the Ellmers house, even though her prints weren't on the gun."

Vanessa smiled.

"It's possible we'll learn that."

"That's what I was afraid to hear. Is she safe now?"

Vanessa gave him an almost imperceptible nod before she leaned into him.

⁂

"I haven't seen my daughter in years. I don't know where she is, and I don't care to."

Detective Allison Kato had to use all her self-restraint not to cringe at those harsh words from Lawrence Mitchell. She felt partly responsible. They had all given Joanna too much leeway. It had been too easy, too intriguing, because she had a way of taking charge.

If she was in any trouble now, that was on her and Theo too.

Allison couldn't help hoping that she'd be on a beach somewhere.

⁂

Rue had decided to take the job offer and start on a part-time basis. Money would be a little tighter, but it was still enough for her, and she wasn't sure how she'd handle a full workday at this point. She tried to gently convince her parents that they should return to their home after being cramped into her guest room for long enough. She still didn't dare say that their presence made *her* feel cramped.

After her first half day, her mother took her out for lunch, to celebrate a small success.

"You know, I'm really grateful you and Dad always accepted me. My former boss, Joanna's dad—growing up with someone like that must be a nightmare."

She didn't even know where that was coming from, now, but her mother was unfazed by the non-sequitur.

"It never occurred to us to do anything else. He seems...cold. Have you heard anything from her?"

Rue shook her head, all of a sudden close to tears.

"No. I don't understand. Vanessa said she was looking for me, but now no one knows where she is. Nothing makes sense."

"She had some troubles of her own to deal with, I imagine. You really liked her, didn't you?"

"I don't know if I was smart or foolish to go for it. Whatever that was, it's over now. I'm still worried something might have happened to her, though Vanessa denies it, and I haven't found anything in the papers or on the Internet."

"What if she doesn't want to be found, by anyone—not even you?"

"Then I'll have to accept that," Rue said even though she was far from it.

Chapter
Twenty-One

F reedom didn't mean the same to everyone. Joanna had a roof over her head, a job that allowed her to make a living, and she hadn't smoked a cigarette in months. She kept to herself and read a lot from the local library.

She had formed a friendship with the owner of the inn that employed her to do the books and the occasional odd job around the house for them.

Here, she was confined to another form of solitude. It wasn't grey walls that fenced her in, but the ocean, and occasionally, her own thoughts.

She was lucky, she knew.

After years of running, denial and raging against her fate, she was coming to terms. The only regrets left were for the people she'd caused pain, but as far as she knew, neither Theo and Allison, nor Vanessa or Kira had faced dire consequences over her disappearance.

Joanna wasn't sure how the man who had brought her here and Vanessa knew one another. He had to be a contact from long before her days at the IAB. Apparently, she trusted him—and he'd come through. The principle was the same as in witness protection, only that Joanna was a witness the police would have liked to talk to.

In the beginning, anyway.

With every day, it became less likely they'd come after her, and for what?

Every once in a while, doubts crept in. What if they had simply told the whole truth? She had assisted her former colleagues in stopping what was an eleven-year killing spree. They couldn't reprimand or fire her from the department. Should she have taken the risk?

Joanna wished she could have taken the time to say goodbye to Rue. No, the truth was, she wished she'd never have to leave her—but it was out of her hands now.

❦

There was an understanding between the two of them that Vanessa had a vague idea of Joanna's whereabouts, but neither of them would bring up the subject in so many words. Seize the moment. Live. Be happy in a bizarre world. At least Vanessa and Theo were trying.

She kept checking up on Rue who had finally managed to convince her parents to move back home.

Other cases came along, and one night Theo was working late, Vanessa decided it was time to take the chance. She knew Rue was back to a functional life. She wasn't happy.

Vanessa wasn't sure if she had the power to make her. She could only try.

She dropped by Rue's condo after work. The woman opening the door to her looked tired. Vanessa could sympathize. Coming back from a traumatic experience like that took hard work, every day.

Christina had begun an outpatient therapy after her release as well. At least, the two of them had escaped the fate of the slasher's other victims.

"Hey. What can I do for you?"

"We need to talk."

"Do we?"

"Can I come in?"

Rue shrugged. "If you must. I'm afraid I can't offer you much. I was going to order in tonight."

"That's fine. I'll invite myself if you don't mind, and don't worry, I'll pay."

"Yeah, whatever."

Rue still lived in the same condo. As she went to the kitchen in search of some takeout flyers, Vanessa took a seat on the couch, wondering if she was doing the right thing. It didn't look like Rue was much interested in change.

What she had to tell her would change everything.

Rue returned with a couple of leaflets and a bottle of wine.

"I don't feel so bad opening this when I have company. Someone at the firm gave it to me as a welcome gift...I was afraid that if I started it by myself, I'd drink the whole bottle."

"I understand."

The look Rue gave her was skeptical, reminding Vanessa of Joanna. True, she had seen some bad stuff that probably couldn't compare.

"You told the whole story," Rue said. "Thank you for that. I had no idea how my prints ended up on the gun. I remember feeling a knife in my hand...but it's all flashes and small parts. I can't come up with the whole picture."

"You don't have to."

"Yeah, maybe."

"You didn't do anything wrong. I was cleared, and...I wanted to tell you I'm leaving IA. It's the better solution anyway, being with Theo."

"Oh. Sure. That makes sense." Rue took two glasses out of the cabinet and poured the wine for both of them. "I'm happy for you...if that's what you want."

"What do *you* want, Rue?"

Rue laughed bitterly.

"My life back? It shouldn't matter so much, after all we didn't know each other that long, but I'd like to know why the hell Joanna never came to see me. I mean...You're not grieving, so I guess she's okay, just doesn't want to talk to me. I know she was mad at me when she found out I worked for her father, but I thought we had put all of that behind us. Hell, I threw my career out of the window...not because of her. It wouldn't be fair to say that. It was a wake-up call, though, when we met...I wanted a clean slate."

Vanessa drank from her glass—and again.

"There's something else you need to know. Joanna didn't exactly have a choice, because I...didn't shoot Short."

"What? Why the hell would you say you did?"

"To share the burden? Look, you can't tell anyone about this, ever. If you did, I'd deny I said it, and they would probably believe me. Your memory is sketchy. You blocked out most of the time during your abduction. Joanna did come for you."

Rue stared at her through wide eyes.

"We made a judgment call, okay? She had already been convicted for a similar situation. What do you think would have happened?"

"All of this...why? You could have told the truth, the whole truth. He was going to kill me. Him, this Decker guy, they loved to kill. Why would anyone doubt her?"

Vanessa felt a flash of uncomfortable heat at the question, and the only answer she had, her own part in what had led them here.

"I couldn't take the chance."

"So, you went ahead and made decisions for all of us."

That was, she had to admit, a just description of the events.

"No matter how much we understand these feelings, we can't have cops running around, being judge, jury, and executioner. It doesn't work that way."

Rue pulled up her legs under herself and studied Vanessa with curiosity.

"Then what works? They like to hurt and kill women. Again, and again. Prison doesn't stop them from thinking they have the right, it doesn't stop the fantasies."

"I'm aware of that."

Joanna had once asked her the same questions, shortly before her arrest.

Vanessa couldn't come up with words that would be enough for each of them, with an answer that was safe for any of them.

There was one thing she could do.

"How attached are you—to this place, your new job, friends in town?"

"I don't understand a thing you're saying."

"Do you miss Joanna? Do you think you two could have a future if you could be together?"

Tears were glistening in Rue's eyes. "Now that's just cruel."

"No, it's a chance, but it's the only one you get."

"What if she doesn't want to see me? Damn it, you're all crazy."

"I'm certain she'd love to see you. The thing is I can't just arrange a date for you two. This is it. You can say yes, and leave in a few hours, or you say no and forget we ever had this conversation. I'd understand. Like you said, you haven't known each other for long."

For a long time, Rue didn't say anything, making Vanessa fear for what her answer would be. For her own peace of mind, she wanted to create something good. Help fate along, if she couldn't turn back time to when everything had been so much easier and clearer.

The longing in Rue's expression was unmistakable though.

"It is sunny there, too," Vanessa said.

Decker's widow had called her a cold-blooded killer in court, regardless of her late husband's record. On social media, many people had called her many different names.

The truth was a lot more complicated than that. Somewhere between right and wrong, helpful, hopeful, and hindering necessary progress, there was a grey zone Joanna had inhabited for a long time, because she'd known and feared the moment history repeated itself, like it always did.

Her new life was a lot different from that, the loss of proximity to her old job and the people in it part of a healing process she had never imagined.

Still, she felt a longing that was painful, translating into dreams of a time when Joanna had thought she could have it all.

She stood on the deck of the small house, a beer in hand. It was Friday. She had stopped smoking the moment she'd set foot on this island, and she'd never gone back to vodka. Clarity was a double-edged sword, but it was better than losing herself in a fog. Joanna actually enjoyed her work.

She frowned at the sight of a cab climbing the hill. Since Vanessa's contact had dropped her off and the details about housing and work were determined, she hadn't had visitors.

The only people she saw were tourists at the inn, and she didn't socialize with them. She placed the bottle on the railing and walked down the steps to the driveway. The cab had come to a halt on the edge of the property, and a woman exited from the car.

Impossible.

Rue walked faster, and so did Joanna, until she could close the last bit of distance between them, pulling her close.

It had to be one of those dreams, seductive and cruel at the same time, where Rue was in her arms and she swore to herself she'd get it right this time, no more detours or heroics...

"You're real," Rue said, holding on tight. "Please tell me I didn't do something incredibly stupid. I...I might need a roof over my head."

Joanna kissed her softly.

"I want to say welcome home, but I'm afraid you just came by for a visit. How did you get here?" She took Rue's hand, leading her up to the house.

"Long story. Actually, it's not. Vanessa."

"I figured. You..." She was still afraid of asking the question. "You know everything?" Damn, that was not what she wanted to ask. "You're going to stay?"

"If you'll have me—but I hope you will, because I don't know anyone here, and I don't think I can go back."

"Then don't."

Joanna would never forget the day Rue came back into her life, or the quiet intimacy at the early dawn of the day.

They had faced losses along the way, but in the end, they still won.

203

Kira hadn't shown the postcard to her husband, children, or anyone. Just once in a while, she took it out of the drawer, looked at it, and smiled. Sometimes, people got what they deserved.

About the Author

B arbara Winkes writes sapphic crime drama and Christmas romance. She loves writing characters who get the job done, whether it's stopping a predator or saving cherished traditions—while still making time for love. She lives with her wife in Quebec City.

barbarawinkes.com

Also by Barbara Winkes

Luce Allen Mysteries
In Harm's Way
Under Pressure

The Crossing Lines Trilogy
Undercover
Redemption
Vengeance

The Connected Series
Promised to the Queen
Drawn to the Enemy
Tempted by the Protector
Saved by the Heiress

Carpenter/Harding
Indiscretions
Insinuations
Incisions
Intrusions

BARBARA WINKES

Initiations
Intentions
Infatuations
Impressions
Implications
Infractions
Incidents
Illusions

Kelli & Merin Romantic Suspense
Thunder
Rain

Lord and Burton
Clean Slate

Standalone
The Amnesia Project